D0849123

THE RETURN

ROBERTO BOLAÑO

THE RETURN

Translated by Chris Andrews

A NEW DIRECTIONS BOOK

Translation copyright © 2010 by Chris Andrews

These stories are selected from two volumes originally published by Editorial Anagrama, Barcelona, Spain, *Llamadas telefónicas* (1997) and *Putas asesinas* (2001), and are published by arrangement with the Heirs of Roberto Bolaño and Carmen Balcells Agencia Literaria, Barcelona.

Grateful acknowledgment is made to the magazines where some of these stories originally appeared: *Harper's*, *The New Yorker*, and *Playboy*.

Manufactured in the United States of America
Published simultaneously in Canada by Penguin Books Canada, Ltd.
New Directions Books are printed on acid-free paper.
First published as a New Directions Book in 2010

Library of Congress Cataloging-in-Publication Data

Bolaño, Roberto, 1953–2003.
  The return / Roberto Bolaño ; translated by Chris Andrews.
    p. cm.
  "These stories are selected from two volumes Originally published by Editorial Anagrama, Barcelona, Spain, Llamadas telefonicas (1997) and Putas asesinas (2001)."
  ISBN 978-0-8112-1715-6 (cloth : alk. paper)
  ISBN 978-0-8112-1905-1 (pbk. : alk. paper)
  I. Andrews, Chris, 1962– II. Bolaño, Roberto, 1953–2003 Llamadas telefónicas. III. Bolaño, Roberto, 1953–2003 Putas asesinas. IV. Title.
  PQ8098.12.O38R48   2010
  863'.64—DC22   2010008155

10 9 8 7 6 5 4 3 2 1

New Directions Books are published for James Laughlin
by New Directions Publishing Corporation,
80 Eighth Avenue, New York 10011

CONTENTS

THE RETURN

SNOW

I met him in a bar on Calle Tallers, in Barcelona, it must be about five years ago now. When he found out I was Chilean, he came over to say hello; he too had been born in that faraway place.

He was more or less the same age as me, thirty-odd, and he drank quite a bit, though I never saw him drunk. His name was Rogelio Estrada. He was thin, shortish, and dark. His smile seemed to be permanently poised between wonder and mischief, but after a while I discovered that he was far more innocent than he made out. One night I went to the bar with a group of Catalan friends. We got talking about books. Rogelio came over to our table and said that the greatest writer of the century was, without a doubt, Mikhail Bulgakov. One of the Catalans had read *The Master and Margarita* and *A Theatrical Novel*, but Rogelio mentioned other works by the distinguished novelist, more than ten of them, if I remember correctly, and he gave their titles in Russian. My friends and I thought he was joking, and soon the talk moved on. One night he invited me back to his place and I went, I don't know why. He lived in a street nearby, a few yards from a very decrepit movie theater known to the local kids as the Ghost Cinema. The apartment was old and full of furniture that wasn't his. We sat down in the living room, Rogelio put on a record—some awful, emphatic music with an unrelenting crescendo—and then he filled two glasses with vodka. On a shelf, presiding over the room, was a silver-framed photo of a girl. The rest of the decor was nothing special: postcards from various European countries and some very old shabby-looking soccer pennants: Colo-Colo, University of Chile and Santiago Morning. Pretty, isn't she? said Rogelio, pointing at the girl in the silver frame. Yes, very pretty, I replied. Then we sat down again and drank for a while in silence. When Rogelio eventually spoke, the bottle was almost empty. First you have to empty the bottle, he said, then your soul. I shrugged. Though, of course, I don't believe in the soul, he added. It all comes down to time, though, doesn't it? Do you have time to listen to my story? Depends on the story, I said, but I think so. It won't take very long, said Rogelio. Then he stood up, took the silver-framed photo, sat down in front of me cradling it in his left arm while holding the glass of vodka in his right hand, and began:

My childhood was happy; it had nothing to do with the way my life turned out later. Things started going wrong when I was a teenager. I was living in Santiago with my family and according to my father I was well on the way to becoming a juvenile delinquent. My father, in case you don't know (and I can't see why you would), was José Estrada Martínez, aka Chubby Estrada, one of the big wheels in the Chilean Communist Party. And we were a proudly proletarian family, fighting the good fight, upstanding and righteous. At the age of thirteen I stole a bicycle. You can imagine, I don't need to spell it out. I was caught two days later and got one hell of a thrashing. At fourteen I started smoking dope—some of my friends in the neighborhood used to grow it in the foothills of the Andes. At the time my father had a senior position in Allende's government, and his biggest fear, poor old dad, was that the right-wing press would reveal the misdemeanors of his eldest son. At fifteen I stole a car. I wasn't caught (though now I know that with a bit more time, the cops would have found me) because a few days later the coup happened and my whole family took refuge in the Soviet Embassy. I don't need to tell you what the days I spent in there were like. It was awful. I slept in the corridor and kept trying to hit on the daughter of one of my father's comrades, but all they did, that bunch, was sing *The International* or *No pasarán*. You get the picture, it was dismal, like party time at the Bible Hall.

We arrived in Moscow at the beginning of 1974. Personally, to be honest, I was glad to be going: a new city, blonde blue-eyed Russian girls, the plane trip, Europe, a new culture. The reality turned out quite differently. Moscow was like Santiago, but quieter, bigger and brutally cold in winter. At first they put me in a school where it was Spanish half the time, Russian the other half. Two years later I was at a regular school, speaking okay Russian, and bored out of my wits. I guess some strings were pulled to get me into the University, because I really didn't study much. I enrolled in medicine, but dropped out after a semester; it wasn't for me. Still, I have good memories of my time there: it's where I made my first friend, I mean the first friend who wasn't an exiled Chilean like me. His name was Jimmy Fodeba and he came from the Central African Republic, which as the name suggests, is in the middle of Africa. Jimmy's father was a communist, like mine, and like my father, he'd been forced into exile. Jimmy was pretty smart, but underneath he was just like me. I mean, he liked to stay up late, he liked to drink and smoke the occasional joint, and he liked women. Before long we were joined at the hip. The best friend I've ever had, except for the gang back in Santiago, the guys who stayed—I'll probably never see them again, but who knows? Anyway, what happened was that Jimmy and I combined our forces, and our desires, and, while we were at it, our needs as well, and from then on, instead of being two separate exiles, feeling lost and lonely, we were a pair of wolves roaming the streets of Moscow, and whenever one of us was scared, the other one dared, and so, little by little (because sometimes Jimmy had to study, he was a good student, unlike me), we started to get a general idea of the city where both of us would probably be living for a fair while. I won't go on about our youthful adventures, all I'll say is that after a year we knew where to find a bit of weed, which may not seem like much of a feat now, in Barcelona, but in Moscow, back in those days, it was truly heroic. By then I'd tried studying Latin American literature, Russian literature, radio broadcasting, food science, just about everything really, and whether it was because I got bored, or didn't pay attention in class, or just didn't turn up, which is basically what happened most of the time, I failed everything, and eventually my father threatened to send me to work in a factory in Siberia, poor old guy, that's the way he was.

And that was how I came to enroll in the School of Physical Education, which some optimistic Russians used to call the Advanced School of Physical Education, and this time I managed to keep it together until I got my diploma. That's right, my friend, you're looking at a qualified gymnastics instructor. Not a good one, of course, especially not compared with some of the Russians, but qualified all the same. When

I handed my father the diploma, the old man was moved to tears. I'd say that's when my adolescence came to an end.

At the time I used to call myself Roger Strada. I was always getting into trouble; my friends weren't what you'd call good, upstanding citizens and I was thoroughly bad. It was like I was full of rage and didn't know how to get it out of my system. I worked as a trainer's assistant for a man of dubious and disconcerting moral character (it was a true meeting of minds); he specialized in recruiting new athletes from secondary schools, and I spent most of my time at parties, making deals and doing shady business to supplement my salary. My boss was called Pultakov. He was divorced and lived in a tiny apartment in Leliushenko Street, near Rogachev Square. As I said, I was a bad boy and Jimmy Fodeba was bad too, and anyone who knew us well knew that we were bad (I think I chose to call myself Roger, at least for a start, because it went with Jimmy, and because I secretly thought of myself as a kind of Italian-American gangster), but Pultakov was *seriously* bad and working with him every day, I gradually came to discover all his tricks, depravities and vices. My father lived in a Moscow of papers and memoranda, a bureaucrats' Moscow, with its commands and countermands, its current issues, its factions and infighting: an ideal Moscow. I lived in a Moscow of drugs and prostitution, black marketeering and living it up, threats and crimes. In certain circles the two Moscows would occasionally come into contact and even intermingle, but as a rule they were two distinct cities, each unaware of the other's existence. Pultakov initiated me into the world of sports betting. We gambled with other people's money of course, but also with our own. Soccer, hockey, basketball, boxing, even championship skiing, a sport I've never really seen the attraction of: we dabbled in everything. I met people. All sorts of people. Nice enough guys, in general, small-time crooks like me, though sometimes I did come across real criminals, the sort who'd stop at nothing, or at least you could tell that *in certain circumstances* they'd stop at nothing. An instinct for survival prevented me from getting too close to those people. Prison-fodder, sewer-food. People who could intimidate Pultakov and terrify me and Jimmy. With one exception, a guy our age, who for some reason took a shine to me. His name was Misha Semionovich Pavlov and he was like the whiz kid of the Moscow underworld. Pultakov and I provided him with information about various sports for his gambling, and from time to time this Misha Pavlov invited us to his apartment, or one of his apartments, never the same one, all of them dingier than Pultakov's or mine, usually out in the old northeastern suburbs, where the workers lived: Poluboyarov, Viktoria and Old Market. Pultakov didn't like Pavlov (he didn't like anyone much) and tried to keep his dealings with him to a minimum, but I've always been naïve; Pavlov's reputation as the underworld's child prodigy and the thoughtful way he treated me—occasionally giving me a chicken or a bottle of vodka or a pair of shoes—finally won me over, and I succumbed completely, body and soul, as they say.

The years went by and my family returned to Chile, except for my younger sister, who married a Russian; my father died in Santiago and had a beautiful funeral, or so they told me in the letters; Jimmy Fodeba went on living in Moscow and working in a hospital (his father went back to the Central African Republic, where he was killed), while Pultakov and I went scurrying like a pair of rats around the gyms and sports complexes. With the arrival of democracy and the end of the

Soviet Union (not that I've ever been interested in politics) came freedom and the mafias. Moscow became a charming, exuberant city, buzzing with that fierce, typically Russian sort of exuberance. I can't explain it, you have to understand the Slavic soul, and I don't think you do, however many books you've read. Suddenly it all got too big for us. Pultakov, who was a Stalinist at heart (I still don't get that, because under Stalin he would have ended up in Siberia for sure), was nostalgic for the old days. But I adapted to the new situation, and decided to save some money, now that it was possible, so I could get out of there for good and start exploring the world, Europe to begin with, then Africa, which, in spite of my age—by then I was over thirty and old enough to know better—I imagined as the kingdom of adventure, an endless frontier, a new story book where I could begin again, be happy, and find myself, as we used to say when we were kids back in Santiago in 1973. And that was how I joined Misha Pavlov's staff, almost without realizing it. At the time his nickname was Billy the Kid. Don't ask me why. Billy the Kid was quick on the draw; Misha never did anything quickly, not even pulling out his credit card. Billy the Kid was brave and, at least in the movies I've seen, agile and thin; Misha was brave too, but built like a Buddha, obese even by Russian standards, and allergic to all forms of physical exercise. I went on being a bookmaker, but soon I began to do other kinds of work for him. Sometimes he'd give me a bundle of cash and send me to see a player I knew to get him to throw a game. On one occasion I managed to bribe half a soccer team, one by one, flattering the more cooperative players and using veiled threats on the others. Sometimes he sent me to persuade other gamblers to withdraw their bets or not to make waves. But most of the time my work consisted of providing reports on athletes, one after another, without any evident rhyme or reason, which Pavlov's IT expert would tirelessly key into his computer.

There was, however, something else I used to do for him. Most of the Moscow gangsters' girls were nightclub hostesses or striptease artists, actresses or wannabes. No surprises there; that's the way it's always been. But Pavlov's taste in women was for athletes: long jumpers, sprinters, middle-distance runners, triple jumpers . . . he fell in love with the occasional javelin thrower, but his real favorites were the high jumpers. He said they were like gazelles, ideal women, and he wasn't wrong. I was the one who organized it all. I went to the training camps and set up dates for him. Some of the girls were delighted at the prospect of spending a weekend with Misha Pavlov, poor things, but others, most of them, weren't. Still, I always got him the girls he wanted, even if it meant spending my own money or resorting to threats. And so it happened that one afternoon he told me he wanted Natalia Mijailovna Chuikova, an eighteen-year-old from the Volgograd region, who had just arrived n Moscow, hoping to get a place on the Olympic team. I don't know what it was exactly, but right from the start I realized that there was something different in the way Pavlov was talking about this Chuikova girl. When he told me to get her, he was with two of his buddies, and they winked at me as if to say: Make sure you do exactly what he's telling you, Roger Strada, because this time Billy the Kid is serious.

Two days later I got to talk to Natalia Chuikova. It was at the Spartanovka indoor track, on the Boulevard of Sport, at nine a.m., and I'm definitely not a morning person, but it was the only time I could meet her there. First I saw her in the distance: she was about to start running to the high jump, and she was concentrating, clenching her fists and looking up, as if she was praying or watching for an angel. Then I went over to her and introduced myself. Roger Strada? she said, So you must be Italian. I didn't have the courage to destroy her illusions altogether: I said I was Chilean and that there were lots of Italians in Chile. She was five-foot-ten and can't have weighed more than 120 pounds. She had long brown hair, and her simple ponytail gathered all the grace in the world. Her eyes were almost jet black and she had, I swear, the longest, most beautiful legs I have ever seen.

I couldn't bring myself to tell her the reason for my visit. I bought her a Pepsi, told her I liked her technique and left. That night I didn't know what I was going to say to Pavlov, what lie I was going to invent. In the end I decided to keep it simple. I said we'd have to give Natalia Chuikova a little time, she wasn't like his usual kind of girl. Misha looked at me with that face of his, somewhere between a seal and a spoiled child, and said OK, I'll give you three days. When Misha gave you three days, you had to fix it in three days, not one day more. So I spent a few hours thinking it over, asking myself what my problem was, what was holding me back, and eventually I decided to settle the matter as quickly as possible. Very early the next morning, I saw Natalia again. I was one of the first to arrive at the track. I spent a long time watching the athletes coming and going, all half asleep like me, chatting and arguing, though all I could hear of their voices was a senseless murmur, or shouts in an incomprehensible Russian, as if I'd forgotten the language, until Natalia appeared in the group and started doing warm-up exercises. Her trainer was taking notes in a little book. There were two other high jumpers talking with her.

Sometimes they laughed. Sometimes, after jumping, they'd sit down and put on blue and red tracksuits, which they soon took off again. Sometimes they drank water. After half an hour of happiness I realized I was in love. It was the first time it had happened to me. Before that, I'd loved a couple of whores. I'd treated them wrong, or right, it didn't matter. Now I was really in love. I spoke to her. I explained the situation with Misha Pavlov, who he was, what he wanted. Natalia was shocked, then she thought it was funny. She agreed to see him, against my advice. I made the date for as late as I could. In the meantime, I took her to see a Bruce Willis movie—he was one of her favorite actors—and then to dinner at a good restaurant. We talked and talked. Her life, with its hardships and disappointments, was a model of perseverance and willpower, just the opposite of mine. Her tastes were simple; it was happiness she wanted, not wealth. Her attitude to sex, which is what I was really hoping to get out of her, was broad-minded. That depressed me at first: I thought Natalia would be easy game for Pavlov, I imagined her sleeping with all his bodyguards, one by one, and I couldn't bear the thought of it. But then I understood that Natalia was talking about a kind of sexuality that I just didn't understand (and still don't), and it didn't mean she had to go to bed with all the gang. I also understood that in spite of everything, I had to protect her.

A week later Pavlov sent me back to the indoor track with a big bunch of red and white carnations that must have cost him an arm and a leg. Natalia took the flowers and asked me to wait for her. We spent the whole day together, downtown for a start (where I bought two novels by Bulgakov, her favorite writer, from a stall in Staraya Basmannaya Street) and then in the little room where she lived. I asked her if she'd had a good time. Her reply completely stunned me, I swear. She said the flowers were self-explanatory. It was just so hard, so cold, you know what I mean: she was Russian and I was Chilean, it was like a chasm was opening in front of me, and I burst into tears right there and then. I often think about that afternoon of crying and how it changed my life. I don't know how to explain it; all I know is I felt like a child, and I felt all the cold of Moscow for the first time, and it seemed unbearable. That afternoon we made love.

From then on my life was in Natalia's hands and her life was in the hands of Misha Pavlov. The situation, in itself, seemed simple enough, but knowing Pavlov I knew that by sleeping with Natalia I was risking my neck. Also, as the days went by, the certitude that Natalia was sleeping with Pavlov— and I knew exactly when she was—progressively embittered and depressed me, and led me to take a fatalistic view of my life, and of life in general. I would have liked to talk it over with a friend and get it off my chest. But no way could I tell Pultakov, and Jimmy Fodeba was always really busy; we weren't seeing each other as often as before. All I could do was put up with it and wait.

And so a year went by.

Life with Pavlov was strange. His life was divided into at least three parts and I had the honor or the misfortune of being acquainted with all three: the life of Pavlov the businessman, continually surrounded by his bodyguards, which gave off a subtle odor of money and blood that unsettled the senses; the life of Pavlov the serial romantic, or lech, as we used to say in Santiago, which tormented me in particular and inflamed my imagination; and the life of Pavlov the private man, with his inquiring mind, a man who spent or wanted to spend his spare time, his "moments of inner repose" as he said, exploring literature and the arts, because Pavlov, though it's hard to believe, was a keen reader, and, of course, he liked to talk about what he was reading. That was why he used to call on the three people who made up what you might call the cultural or cosmopolitan arm of his gang: Fedor Petrovich Semionov, a novelist; Paulo Ripellino, a genuine Italian, who was studying Russian on a scholarship from the Moscow School of Languages; and me, who he always introduced as his friend Roger Strada, though he sometimes treated me like a dog. Two Russians and two Italians, Pavlov would say, with a little smile on his lips. He did it to slight me in front of Ripellino, but Ripellino was always respectful to me. They were actually fun, those meetings, but sometimes we'd be summoned at midnight; the phone would ring and we'd have to get ourselves pronto to one of the many apartments Pavlov owned around Moscow, and endure the boss's rants, when all we wanted to do was to go to bed. Pavlov's tastes were eclectic—that's the word, isn't it? The only author I've read, to be honest, is Bulgakov, and that was only because I was in love with Natalia; as for the others, I've got no idea, I'm not much of a reader, that's pretty obvious. Semionov, as far as I know, wrote pornographic novels, and Ripellino had a film script that he wanted Pavlov to back for him, something about martial arts and the mafia. The only one who really knew about literature was our host. So Pavlov would start talking about Dostoyevsky, for example, and the rest of us would tag along. The next day I'd take myself to the library and look up information about Dostoyevsky, summaries of his works and his life, so I'd have something to say the next time, but Pavlov hardly ever repeated himself; one week he'd talk about Dostoyevsky, the next about Boris Pilniak, the week after that,

Chekhov (who he said was a faggot, I don't know why), then he'd be onto Gogol or Semionov himself, raving about his pornographic novels. Semionov was quite a character. He must have been my age, maybe a bit older, and he was one of Pavlov's protégés. I once heard that he'd arranged for his wife to disappear. I didn't know what to think about that rumor. Semionov seemed capable of anything, except biting the hand that fed him. Ripellino was different, a good kid, and the only one who openly confessed that he hadn't read a single one of the novelists that our boss used to hold forth about, although he'd read some poetry (Russian poetry, with proper rhymes, easy to remember), which he'd sometimes recite by heart, usually when we were drunk. And who wrote that? Semionov would ask in a booming voice. Pushkin, who else? Ripellino would reply. Then I'd seize the opportunity to say my piece about Dostoyevsky, and Pavlov and Ripellino would recite Pushkin's poem in unison, and Semionov would get out a little book and pretend to be taking notes for his next novel. Or we'd talk about the Slavic soul and the Latin soul, and once we got onto that subject, of course, Ripellino and I were bound to come off badly. You can't imagine how long Pavlov could go on about the Slavic soul, how profound and sad he could get. Semionov usually ended up crying, and Ripellino and I backed down at the first sign of trouble. It wasn't always just the four of us, of course. Sometimes Pavlov sent out for some whores. Sometimes there'd be one or two unfamiliar faces: the editor of a little magazine, an out-of-work actor, a retired army officer who actually knew the complete works of Alexei Tolstoy. Pleasant or unpleasant company, people who were doing deals with Pavlov or hoping for a favor from him. Sometimes the night even turned out to be enjoyable. But it could go the other way too. I'll never understand the Slavic soul. One night Pavlov showed his guests some photos of what he called his "women's high-jumping team." At first I didn't want to look, but they called me over and I couldn't refuse. There were photos of the four or five high-jumpers I'd gotten for him. Natalia Chuikova was one of them. I felt ill and I think Pavlov realized; he put his massive arms around me and started singing a drinking song in my ear, something about death and love, the only two things in life that are real. I remember laughing or trying to laugh at Pavlov's little joke, like I always did, but the laughter died in my throat. Later, when the others were sleeping it off, or had gone, I sat down by the window and looked at the photos again, taking my time. Funny how it is: right then, everything seemed OK, all in order (as my father used to say), I was breathing deeply, calm, free. It also seemed to me that the Slavic soul was not so different from the Latin soul, in fact they were the same, and the same as the African soul, which presumably illuminated the nights of my friend Jimmy Fodeba. Maybe the Slavic soul could withstand more alcohol, but that was the only difference.

So time went by.

Natalia was dropped from the Olympic team because she never managed to jump the required height. She competed in the national trials and wasn't highly ranked. It was clear that she wouldn't be breaking any records. Although she didn't want to admit it, her career was over, and sometimes we talked about the future with a mixture of fear and anticipation. Her relationship with Pavlov had its ups and downs; there were days when he seemed to love her more than anyone in the world and days when he treated her badly. One night when we met her face was covered with bruises. She told me it had happened at training, but I knew it was Pavlov. Sometimes we talked late into the night about travel and other countries. I told her stuff about Chile, a Chile of my own invention, I guess, which sounded a lot like Russia to her, so she couldn't get excited about it, but she was curious. Once she travelled to Italy and Spain with Pavlov. They didn't invite me to the send-off, but I was one of the people who went to the airport to welcome them home. Natalia returned looking very tanned and pretty. I gave her a bunch of white roses (the night before, Pavlov had called from Spain and told me to buy them). Thanks, Roger, she said. You're welcome, Natalia Mijailovna, I said, instead of confessing that it was all thanks to a long-distance phone call from our mutual boss. Right then he was talking with some heavies and didn't notice the tenderness in my eyes (which have often been compared to the eyes of a rat, even by my mother, God rest her soul). But the fact is that Natalia and I were letting our guard down.

One winter night Pavlov called me at home. He sounded furious. He ordered me to come and see him immediately. I'd heard through the grapevine that some of his business operations weren't going so well. I tried to suggest that maybe it could wait, given the time and the temperature outside, but Misha wasn't in a waiting mood: Either you get here in half an hour, he said, or tomorrow morning I cut your balls off. I got dressed as fast as I could and before going out I put a knife in my pocket, a knife I'd bought when I was a medical student. The streets of Moscow, at four in the morning, are not exactly safe, as I guess you know. The trip was like the continuation of the nightmare I'd been having when I was woken by Pavlov's call. The streets were covered with snow, the temperature must have been about five or ten degrees and for quite a while I didn't see another human being. At first I was walking ten yards and then trotting the next ten to warm myself up. After fifteen minutes, my body resigned itself to plodding on, step by step, clenched against the cold. Twice I saw patrol cars coming, and hid. Twice I saw taxis, but neither of them stopped for me. Apart from that, I came across drunks, who ignored me, and shadows, which, as I passed, disappeared into the enormous entrances along Medveditsa Avenue. The apartment where I was to meet Pavlov was in Nemetskaya Street; normally, on foot, it would have taken thirty or thirty-five minutes to get there, but that hellish night it took almost an hour and when I arrived four toes on my left foot were frozen.

Pavlov was waiting for me by the fireplace, reading and drinking cognac. Before I could say anything he smashed his fist into my nose. I hardly felt the blow but I let myself fall anyway. Don't stain my carpet, I heard him say. He proceeded to kick me about five times in the ribs, but since he was wearing slippers, that didn't hurt too much either. Then he took a seat, picked up his book and his glass and seemed to calm down. I got up, went to the bathroom to wash away the blood that was running from my nose, and then returned to the living room. What are you reading? I asked him. Bulgakov, said Pavlov. You know his work, don't you? Ah, Bulgakov, I said as my stomach tied itself in a knot. You mention Natalia, I thought, and I'll kill you. I slipped my hand into my coat pocket, feeling for the little knife. I like sincere people, said Pavlov, honorable people, who aren't underhanded; when I place my trust in someone, I want to be able to trust that person implicitly. My foot is frozen, I said, you should drop me at the hospital. Pavlov didn't listen, so I decided to stop complaining, anyway it wasn't that bad, I could already move my toes. For a while both of us were silent: Pavlov looked at the book by Bulgakov (*The Fateful Eggs*, I think it was), while I watched the flames in the fireplace. Natalia told me you've been seeing her, said Pavlov. I didn't say anything but I nodded. Are you sleeping with that whore? No, I lied. Another silence. Suddenly I was convinced that Pavlov had murdered Natalia and was going to murder me the same night. Without weighing up the consequences I threw myself at him and slashed his throat. I spent the next half hour covering my tracks. Then I went home and got drunk.

A week later the police arrested me and took me to the Ilininkov police station where I was questioned for an hour. A pure formality. Pavlov's replacement was called Igor Borisovich Protopopov, also known as the Sardine. He wasn't interested in athletes, but he kept me on as a bettor and match-fixer. I served him for six months before leaving Russia. What about Natalia, you must be wondering. I saw her the day after killing Pavlov, very early, at the sports center where she trained. She didn't like the look of me. She said I looked like I was dead. I detected a note of scorn in her voice, but also a note of familiarity, even affection. I laughed and said I'd drunk a lot the night before, that was all. Then I took myself to the hospital where Jimmy Fodeba worked to get my frozen toes checked out. It wasn't really a serious problem, but by greasing a few palms we got them to keep me there for three days; then Jimmy fiddled the admission forms so it turned out that when Pavlov was killed, I had been flat on my back, warmly tucked up and happy as could be.

Like I told you, six months later I left Russia. Natalia came with me. First we lived in Paris and we even talked about getting married. It was the happiest time in my life. So happy that when I think back to it now, it makes me feel ashamed. Then we spent a while in Frankfurt and in Stuttgart, where Natalia had friends and hoped to find a good job. The friends weren't so friendly in the end, and poor Natalia couldn't find steady employment, though she even tried working as a cook in a Russian restaurant. But she was no good at cooking. We hardly ever talked about Pavlov's death. Unlike the police, Natalia thought his own men had done away with him, specifically the Sardine, but I said it must have been a rival gang. Funnily enough, she remembered Pavlov as a gentleman and always spoke warmly of his generosity. I let her go on and laughed to myself. Once I asked her if she was related to General Chuikov, the man who defended Stalingrad, now known as Volgograd. The things you come up with, Roger, she said, of course not. When we'd been living together for a year she left me for a German, by the name of Kurt something or other. She told me she was in love and then she cried, because she felt sorry for me or just because she was happy, I don't know. Come on, that's enough, *mala mujer*, I said to her. She started laughing like she always did when I spoke my language. I started laughing too. We shared a bottle of vodka and said good-bye. After that, when I realized there was nothing to keep me in that German city, I came to Barcelona. I'm working as a gymnastics instructor in a private school. Things aren't going too badly; I sleep with whores and there are two bars where I hang out and have a circle, as they say here. But sometimes, especially at night, I miss Russia, I miss Moscow. It's pretty good here but it's not the same, though if you asked me, I wouldn't be able to say exactly what it is I miss. The joy of just being alive? I don't know. One of these days I'm going to get on a plane and go back to Chile.

ANOTHER RUSSIAN TALE

for Anselmo Sanjuán

Once, after a conversation with a friend about the mercurial nature of art, Amalfitano told a story he'd heard in Barcelona. The story was about a *sorche*, a rookie, in the Spanish Blue Division, which fought in the Second World War, on the Russian Front, with the German Northern Army Group to be precise, in the vicinity of Novgorod.

The rookie was a little guy from Seville, blue-eyed and thin as a rake, and more or less by accident (he was no Dionisio Ridruejo, not even a Tomás Salvador; when he had to give the Roman salute, he did, but he wasn't really a fascist or a Falangist at heart) he ended up in Russia. And there, for some reason, someone started calling him *sorche* for short: Over here, *sorche*, or: *Sorche*, do this, *Sorche*, do that, so the word lodged itself in the guy's head, but in the dark part of his head, and in that capacious and desolate place, with passing time and the daily panicking, it was somehow transformed into *chantre*, cantor. How this happened I don't know, let's just say that some connection dormant since childhood was reactivated, some pleasant memory that had been waiting for its chance to return.

So the Andalusian came to think of himself as being a cantor and having a cantor's duties, although he had no conscious idea of what the word meant, and couldn't have said that it referred to the leader of a church or cathedral choir. And yet, and this is the remarkable thing, by thinking of himself as a cantor, he somehow turned himself into one. During the terrible winter of '41, he took charge of the choir that sang carols while the Russians were hammering the 250th Regiment. He remembered those days as full of noise (muffled, constant noises) and an underground, slightly unfocused joy. They sang, but it was as if the voices were lagging behind or even anticipating the movements of the singers' lips, throats and eyes, which in their own brief but peculiar journeys often slipped into a kind of silent crevice.

The Andalusian carried out his other duties with courage and resignation, although over time, he did become embittered.

He soon paid his dues in blood. One afternoon he was wounded, more or less accidentally, and spent two weeks in the military hospital in Riga, under the care of robust, smiling German women, nursing for the Reich, who couldn't believe the color of his eyes, and some extremely ugly volunteer nurses from Spain, probably sisters or sisters-in-law or distant cousins of José Antonio.

When he was discharged, a confusion occurred that was to have grave consequences for the Andalusian: instead of giving him a ticket to the right destination, they shunted him off to the barracks of an SS battalion two hundred miles from his regiment. There, among Germans, Austrians, Latvians, Lithuanians, Danes, Norwegians and Swedes, all much taller and stronger than him, he tried to explain the confusion in his rudimentary German, but the SS officers brushed him off, and while it was being sorted out, they gave him a broom and made him sweep the barracks, then a bucket and a rag to clean the floor of the enormous rectangular wooden building in which they held, interrogated and tortured prisoners of all sorts.

Not entirely resigned to his lot, but performing his new tasks conscientiously, the Andalusian watched the time go by in his new barracks, where he ate much better than before and was not exposed to any new dangers, since the SS battalion had been stationed well behind the lines, to combat what they called "outlaws." Then, in the dark part of his head, the word *sorche* became legible again. I'm a *sorche*, he said, a rookie, and I should accept my fate. Little by little, the word *chantre* disappeared, although some afternoons, under a limitless sky that filled him with nostalgia for Seville, it resonated still, somewhere, lost in the beyond. Once he heard some German soldiers singing, and he remembered the word; another time there was a boy singing behind a thicket, and again he remembered it, more clearly this time, but when he went around to the other side of the bushes, the boy was gone.

One fine day, what was bound to happen happened. The barracks of the SS battalion came under attack and were captured, some say by a Russian cavalry regiment, though others claim it was a group of partisans. The fighting was brief and the Germans were at a disadvantage from the start. After an hour the Russians found the Andalusian hidden in the rectangular building, wearing the uniform of an SS auxiliary and surrounded by evidence of the atrocities committed there not so long ago. Caught red-handed, so to speak. They attached him to one of the chairs that the SS used for interrogations, with straps on the legs and the armrests, and to every question from the Russians he replied in Spanish that he didn't understand and was just a dogsbody there. He also tried to say it in German, but he barely knew four words of that language and his interrogators knew none at all. After a quick session of slapping and kicking, they went to get a guy who could speak German and was questioning prisoners in another of the rectangular building's cells. Before they came back, the Andalusian heard shots, and knew they were killing some of the SS, which put an end to any hopes he might have had of getting out of there unharmed. And yet, when the shooting stopped, he clung to life again with every fiber of his being. The Russian who knew German asked him what he was doing there, what his job was and his rank. The Andalusian tried to explain, in German, but it was no use. Then the Russians opened his mouth, and with a pair of pincers, which the Germans had used on other body parts, they started pulling and squeezing his tongue. The pain made his eyes water, and he said, or rather shouted, the word *coño*, cunt. The pincers in his mouth distorted the expletive which came out, in his howling voice, as *Kunst*.

The Russian who knew German looked at him in puzzlement. The Andalusian was yelling *Kunst, Kunst* and crying with pain. In German, the word *Kunst* means art, and that was what the bilingual soldier was hearing, and he said, This son of a bitch must be an artist or something. The guys who were torturing the Andalusian removed the pincers along with a little piece of tongue and waited, momentarily hypnotized by the revelation. The word *art*. Art, which soothes the savage beast. And so, like soothed beasts, the Russians took a breather and waited for some kind of signal while the rookie bled from the mouth and swallowed his blood liberally mixed with saliva, and choked. The word *coño* transformed into the word *Kunst*, had saved his life. When he came out of the rectangular building, it was dusk, but the light stabbed at his eyes like midday sun.

They took him away along with the few remaining prisoners, and before long he was able to tell his story to a Russian who knew some Spanish, and he ended up in a prison camp in Siberia while his accidental partners in iniquity were executed. He was in Siberia until well into the fifties. In 1957 he settled in Barcelona. Sometimes he'd open his mouth and cheerfully tell his tales of war. Sometimes he'd open his mouth and show whoever wanted a look the place where a chunk was missing from his tongue. You could hardly see it. The Andalusian explained that over the years it had grown back. Amalfitano didn't know him personally. But when he heard the story, the guy was still living in a janitor's apartment in Barcelona.

WILLIAM BURNS

William Burns, from Ventura, California, told this story to my friend Pancho Monge, a policeman in Santa Teresa, Sonora, who passed it on to me. According to Monge, the North American was a laid-back guy who never lost his cool, a description that seems to be at odds with the following account of the events. In Burns's own words:

It was a dreary time in my life. I was going through a rough patch at work. I was supremely bored, though up till then I'd always been immune to boredom. I was going out with two women. That I do remember clearly. One of them was getting on a bit—she must have been about my age—and the other wasn't much more than a girl. Some days, though, they seemed like two ailing, crotchety old women, and other days like two little girls who just wanted to play. The age difference wasn't so big you'd mistake them for mother and daughter, but almost. Though that's the kind of thing a man can only guess at; you never really know for sure. Anyway, these women had two dogs, a big one and a little one. And I never knew which dog belonged to which woman. They were sharing a house on the outskirts of a town in the mountains where people went for summer vacation. When I mentioned to someone, some friend or acquaintance, that I was going up there for the summer, he told me I should take my fishing rod. But I didn't have a fishing rod. Someone else told me about the stores and the cabins, taking it easy, clearing the mind. But I wasn't going there with the women for a vacation; I was going there to take care of them. Why did they ask me to take care of them? What they told me was that some guy was out to harm them. They called him the killer. When I asked what his motive was, they didn't have an answer, or maybe they preferred to keep me in the dark. So I tried to work it out for myself. They were afraid, they believed they were in danger, and maybe it was all a false alarm. But why should I tell people what to think, especially when they've hired me, and anyway I figured that after a week they'd come around to my point of view. So I went up into the mountains with them and their dogs, and we moved into a little stone-and-timber house full of windows, more windows than I think I've ever seen in the one house, all different sizes and scattered haphazardly. From the outside, the windows gave you the impression that the house had three floors, but in fact there were only two. Inside, especially in the living room and some of the bedrooms on the first floor, they produced a dizzying, exhilarating, maddening effect. In the bedroom I was given there were only two windows, both quite small, one above the other, the top one almost reaching the ceiling, the lower one just over a foot from the floor. Anyway, life up there was pleasant. The older woman wrote every morning, but she didn't shut herself away, like they say writers usually do; she set up her laptop on the living room table. The younger woman spent her time gardening or playing with the dogs or

talking with me. I did most of the cooking, and although I'm
no chef, the women praised the meals I prepared. I could have
gone on living like that for the rest of my life. But one day the
dogs ran away and I went out to look for them. I remember
searching through a wood nearby, armed only with a flash-
light, and peering into the gardens of empty houses. I couldn't
find them anywhere. When I got back to the house, the
women looked at me as if I was to blame for the dogs' disap-
pearance. Then they mentioned a name, the killer's name.
They were the ones who'd been calling him the killer right
from the start. I was skeptical, but I listened to what they had
to say. They talked about high school romances, money trouble, grudges. I couldn't get my head around how both of them
could have had relationships with the same guy in high school,
given the age difference between them. But they didn't want
to say any more. That night, in spite of the reproaches, one
of them came to my room. I didn't switch on the light, I was
half asleep, and I never found out which one it was. When I
woke up, with the first light of dawn, I was alone. That day I
decided to go into town and pay a visit to the guy they were
scared of. I asked them for his address and told them to shut
themselves in the house and not to move until I got back. I
drove down in the older woman's pickup. Just before I got to
town, I saw the dogs in the yard of an old canning plant. They
came over to me looking abashed and wagging their tails. I
put them in the cab of the pickup and drove around the town
for a while, laughing at how worried I'd been the previous
night. Predictably, I found myself approaching the address
the women had given me. Let's say the guy was called Bedloe.
He had a store in the middle of town, a store for vacationers,
where he sold everything from fishing rods to checked shirts

and chocolate bars. For a while I just browsed the shelves. The man looked like a movie actor; he can't have been more than thirty-five. He was strongly built, had dark hair, and was reading a newspaper spread out on the counter. He was wearing canvas pants and a tee shirt. The store must have been doing good business; it was on one of the main streets, which had trams running down it as well as cars. Bedloe's stuff was expensive. For a while I checked out the prices and the stock. As I was leaving, for some reason I had the impression that the poor guy was lost. I hadn't gone more than ten yards when I realized that his dog was following me. I hadn't even seen it in the store: a big black dog, maybe a German Shepherd crossed with something else. I've never owned a dog, I've got no idea what makes the damn things tick, but for whatever reason, Bedloe's dog followed me. I tried to get it to go back to the store, of course, but it paid no attention. So I kept walking toward the pickup, with the dog at my side, and then I heard the whistle. The storekeeper was whistling his dog back. I didn't turn around, but I knew that he had come out looking for us. My reaction was automatic and unthinking: I tried to make sure he didn't see me, or didn't see us. I remember hiding behind a dark red tram, the color of dried blood, with the dog pressed against my legs. Just when I was feeling safely hidden, the tram moved off and the storekeeper saw me from the opposite sidewalk and moved his hands in a gesture that could have meant Grab the dog or Hang the dog or Stay right there till I come over. Which is exactly what I didn't do; I turned around and disappeared into the crowd, while he shouted something like Stop, my dog! Hey buddy, my dog! Why did I behave like that? I don't know. Anyway, the storekeeper's dog followed me submissively to where I'd parked the pickup and as soon as I opened the door, before I had time to react, he jumped in and refused to budge. When they saw me arrive with three dogs, the women said nothing and started playing with all three. The storekeeper's dog seemed to know them from way back. That afternoon, we talked about all sorts of things. I started by telling them about what had happened to me in town, then they talked about their past lives and their work: one had been a teacher, the other a hairdresser, and both had quit their jobs, although from time to time, they said, they looked after kids with problems. At some point, I found myself talking about how the house should be guarded around the clock. The women looked at me and agreed with a smile. I regretted having put it like that. Then we ate. I hadn't prepared the meal that night. The conversation lapsed into silence broken only by the sound of our jaws and teeth working, and the scuffling of the dogs outside as they raced around the house. Later, we started drinking. One of the women, I don't remember which, talked about the roundness of the earth and protection and doctor's voices. My mind was elsewhere, I wasn't following. I guess she was referring to the Indians who had once inhabited those mountain slopes. After a while I couldn't stand it any more, so I got up, cleared the table and shut myself in the kitchen to wash the dishes, but I could hear them even there. When I went back to the living room, the younger woman was lying on the sofa, half covered with a blanket, and the other one was talking about a big city; it was as if she were talking up some big city, saying what a great place it was to live, but in fact she was running it down; I could tell, because every now and then both of them would start sniggering. That was something I never got with those two: their humor. I found them attractive, I liked them, but something about their sense of humor always seemed false and forced. The bottle of whiskey I'd opened after dinner was half empty. That bothered me; I had no intention of getting drunk, and I didn't want them to get drunk and leave me out. So I sat down with them and said that we had to talk a few things over. What things? they asked, pretending to be surprised, or maybe they weren't just pretending. This house has too many weak points, I said. We've got to do something about it. What are they? asked one of the women. OK, I said, and I started by reminding them how far it was from town, how exposed it was, but I soon realized they weren't listening. If I was a dog, I thought resentfully, these women would show me a bit more consideration. Later, after I realized that none of us were feeling sleepy, they started talking about children and their voices made my heart recoil. I have seen terrible, evil things, sights to make a hard man flinch, but listening to the women that night, my heart recoiled so violently it almost disappeared. I tried to butt in, I tried to find out if they were recalling scenes from childhood or talking about real children in the present, but I couldn't. My throat felt like it was full of bandages and cotton swabs. Suddenly, in the middle of that conversation or double monologue, I had a premonition and I started moving stealthily toward one of the windows in the living room, a ridiculous little bull's-eye window, in a corner, too close to the main window to serve any useful purpose. I know that at the last moment the women looked at me and realized that something was happening; all I had time to do was put my finger to my lips, before pulling back the curtain and seeing Bedloe's head, the killer's head, outside. What happened next is hazy. And it's hazy because panic is contagious. The killer, I realized immediately, had started running around the outside of the house. The women and I started running around inside. Two circles: he was looking for a way in, trying to find a window left open, while the women and I went around checking the doors and shutting the windows. I know I didn't do what I should have done: gone to my room, got my gun, gone outside and made him surrender. Instead I found myself thinking that the dogs were still out there, and hoping nothing bad would happen to them; one of the dogs was pregnant, I think, I'm not sure—there'd been some talk about it. Anyway, just at that moment, while I was still running around, I heard one of the women say, Jesus, the dog, the dog, and I thought of telepathy, I thought of happiness, and I was afraid that the woman who had spoken, whichever one it was, would go out to look for the dog. Luckily, neither of them made any move to leave the house. Just as well. Just as well, I thought. And then (I'll never forget this) I went into a room on the first floor where I'd never been before. It was long, narrow and dark, illuminated only by the moon and by a faint glow coming from the porch lights. And at that moment I knew, with a terror-driven certitude, that destiny (or misfortune—the same thing in this case) had brought me to that room. At the far end, outside a window, I saw the storekeeper's silhouette. I crouched down, barely able to contain my shaking (my whole body was shaking, the sweat was pouring off me) and waited. The killer opened the window with bewildering ease and slipped quietly into the room. There were three narrow wooden beds each with a bedside table. On the wall, inches above the beds I could see three framed prints. The killer stopped for a moment. I felt him breathe; the air made a healthy sound as it went into his lungs. Then he groped his way forward, between the wall and the feet of the beds, directly toward where I was crouched, waiting for him. Although it was hard to believe, I knew he hadn't seen me: I thanked my lucky stars, and, when he got close enough, I grabbed him by the feet and pulled him down. Once he was on the floor I started kicking him with the aim of doing as much damage as possible. He's here, he's here, I shouted, but the women didn't respond (I couldn't hear them running around either), and the unfamiliar room was like a projection of my brain, the only home, the only shelter. I don't know how long I was in there, kicking that fallen body, I only remember someone opening the door behind me, words I couldn't understand, a hand on my shoulder. Then I was alone again and I stopped kicking him. For a few moments I didn't know what to do; I felt dazed and tired. Eventually, I snapped out of it and dragged the body to the living room. There I found the women, sitting very close together on the sofa, almost hugging each other. I don't know why, but something about the scene made me think of a birthday party. I could see the anxiety in their eyes, and a fading trace of the fear caused not by the episode as a whole but by the sight of Bedloe's body after the beating I'd given him. And it was the look in their eyes that made me lose my grip and let his body drop onto the carpet. Bedloe's face was a blood-spattered mask, garish in the light of the living room. Where his nose had been there was just a bleeding pulp. I checked to see if his heart was beating. The women were watching me without making the slightest movement. He's dead, I said. Before I went out onto the porch, I heard one of them sigh. I smoked a cigarette looking at the stars, thinking about how I'd explain it to the authorities in town. When I went back inside, the women were down on all fours stripping the body and I couldn't stifle a cry. They didn't even look at me. I think I drank a glass of whiskey and then went out again, taking the bottle, I think. I don't know how long I was out there, smoking and drinking, giving the women time to finish their task. I went back over the events, piecing them together. I remembered the man looking in through the window, I remembered the look in his eyes, and now I recognized the fear, I remembered when he lost his dog, and finally I remembered him reading a newspaper at the back of the store. I also remembered the light the previous day, the light inside the store and the porch light seen from the room where I'd killed him. Then I started watching the dogs, who weren't sleeping, either, but running from one end of the yard to the other. The wooden fence was broken in places; someone would have to fix it some day, but it wasn't going to be me. Day began to dawn on the other side of the mountains. The dogs came up onto the porch looking for a pat, probably tired after a long night of playing. Just the usual two. I whistled for the other one, but he didn't come. The revelation struck me with the first shiver of cold. The dead man was no killer. We'd been tricked by the real killer, hidden somewhere far away, or, more likely, by fate. Bedloe didn't want to kill anyone—he was just looking for his dog. Poor bastard, I thought. The dogs went back to chasing each other around the yard. I opened the door and looked at the women, unable to bring myself to go into the living room. Bedloe's body was clothed again. Better dressed than before. I was going to say something, but there was no point, so I went back to the porch. One of the women followed me out. Now we have to get rid of the body, she said behind me. Yes, I said. Later I helped to put Bedloe into the back of the pickup. We drove into the mountains. Life is meaningless, said the older woman. I didn't answer; I dug a grave. When we got back, while they were taking a shower, I washed the pickup and got my stuff together. What will you do now? they asked while we were having breakfast on the porch, watching the clouds. I'll go back to the city, I said, and I'll pick up the investigation exactly where I got off track.

And the end of the story, as Pancho Monge tells it, is that six months later William Burns was killed by unidentified assailants.

DETECTIVES

What kind of weapons do you like?"

"Any kind, except for blades."

"You mean knives, razors, daggers, *corvos*, switchblades, penknives, that sort of thing?"

"Yeah, more or less."

"What do you mean, more or less?"

"It's just a figure of speech, asshole. I don't like any of that stuff."

"You sure?"

"Yes, I'm sure."

"But how can you not like *corvos*?"

"I just don't, that's all."

"But you're talking about our national weapon."

"So the *corvo* is Chile's national weapon?"

"Knives in general, I mean."

"Come off it, compadre."

"I swear to God, I read it in an article the other day. Chileans don't like firearms, it must be because of the noise; we're silent by nature."

"That must be because of the sea."

"How do you mean? What sea?"

"The Pacific, of course."

"Oh, you mean the *ocean*. And what's the Pacific Ocean got to do with silence?"

"They say it absorbs noises, useless noises, I mean. I don't know whether there's anything to it."

"So what about the Argentineans?"

"What have they got to do with the Pacific?"

"Well, they've got the Atlantic and they're pretty noisy."

"But there's no comparison."

"You're right about that, there's no comparison—but Argentineans like knives as well."

"That's exactly why I don't. Even if they're the national weapon. I could make an exception, maybe, for penknives, especially Swiss Army knives, but the rest are just a curse."

"And why's that, compadre? Come on, explain."

"I don't have an explanation, compadre, sorry. That's just how it is, period; it's a gut feeling."

"OK, I see where you're going with this."

"Do you? Better tell me then, because I don't know myself."

"Well, I know, but I don't know how to explain it."

"Mind you, the knife thing does have its advantages."

"Like what, for example?"

"Well, imagine a gang of thieves armed with automatic rifles. Just an example. Or pimps with Uzis."

"OK, I'm following you."

"So you see the advantage?"

"Absolutely, for us. But that's an insult to Chile, you know, that argument."

"An insult to Chile! What?"

"It's an insult to the Chilean character, the way we are, our collective dreams. It's like being told that all we're good for is suffering. I don't know if you follow me, but I feel like I just saw the light."

"I follow you, but that's not it."

"What do you mean, that's not it?"

"That's not what I was talking about. I just don't like knives, period. It's not some big philosophical question."

"But you'd like guns to be more popular in Chile. Which doesn't mean you'd like there to be more of them."

"I don't care one way or the other."

"Anyway, who doesn't like guns?"

"That's true, everyone likes guns."

"Do you want me to explain what I meant about the silence?"

"Sure, as long as you don't put me to sleep."

"I won't, and if you start feeling sleepy, we can stop and I'll drive."

"So tell me about the silence then."

"I read it in an article in *El Mercurio*."

"When did you start reading *El Mercurio*?"

"Sometimes there's a copy lying round at headquarters, and the shifts are long. Anyway, the article said we're a Latin people, and Latin people are fixated on knives. Anglo-Saxons, on the other hand, live and die by the gun."

"It all depends."

"Exactly what I thought."

"Until the moment of truth, you never know."

"Exactly what I thought."

"We're slower, you have to admit."

"How do you mean, slower?"

"Slower in every respect. Old-fashioned in a way."

"You call that being slow?"

"We're still using knives, it's like we're stuck in the Bronze Age, while the gringos have moved on to the Iron Age."

"I never liked history."

"Remember when we arrested Chubby Loayza?"

"How could I forget?"

"There, you see—the guy just gave himself up."

"Yeah, and he had an arsenal in that house."

"There, you see."

"So he should have put up a fight."

"There were only four of us, and five of them. We just had standard issue weapons and Chubby had an arsenal, including a bazooka."

"It wasn't a bazooka, compadre."

"It was a Franchi SPAS-15! And he had a pair of sawn-off shotguns. But Loayza gave himself up without firing a shot."

"So you were disappointed, were you?"

"Or course not. But if he'd been called McCurly instead of Loayza, Chubby would have greeted us with a hail of bullets, and maybe he wouldn't be in jail now."

"Maybe he'd be dead."

"Or free, if you get my drift."

"McCurly? . . . the name rings a bell; wasn't he in a cowboy movie?"

"I think he was, I think we even saw it together."

"We haven't been to the movies together for ages."

"Well, this would have been ages ago."

"The arsenal he had, Chubby Loayza; remember how he greeted us?"

"Laughing his head off."

"I think it was nerves. One of his gang started crying. I don't think that kid was even seventeen."

"But Chubby Loayza was over forty and he made himself out to be a tough guy. Though if we're going to be brutally honest, there aren't any tough guys in this country."

"What do you mean there aren't any tough guys, I've seen really tough guys."

"Crazies, for sure, you've seen plenty of them, but tough guys? Very few, or none."

"And what about Raulito Sánchez? Remember Raulito Sánchez, with his Manurhin?"

"How could I forget him?"

"What about him then?"

"Well, he should have got rid of the revolver straightaway. That was his downfall. Nothing's easier to trace than a Magnum."

"The Manurhin is a Magnum?"

"Of course it's a Magnum."

"I thought it was a French gun."

"It's a .357 French Magnum. That's why he didn't get rid of it. It's an expensive piece and he'd gotten fond of it; there aren't many in Chile."

"You learn something new every day."

"Poor Raulito Sánchez."

"They say he died in jail."

"No, he died just after getting out, in a boarding house in Arica."

"They say his lungs were ruined."

"He'd been spitting blood since he was a kid, but he was brave, he never complained."

"I remember he was very quiet."

"Quiet and hard-working, but a bit too attached to material possessions. That Manurhin was his downfall."

"Whores were his downfall."

"Come on, Raulito Sánchez was a faggot."

"You're kidding! I had no idea. Nothing's sacred. Time levels even the tallest towers."

"Give me a break, what's it got to do with towers?"

"It's just that I remember him as really manly, if you know what I mean."

"What's it got to do with manliness?"

"But he was a man, in his way, though, wasn't he?"

"I don't really know what to say to that."

"I saw him with whores at least once. He didn't turn up his nose at whores."

"He didn't turn up his nose at anyone or anything, but I'm certain he never slept with a woman."

"That's a very definite assertion, compadre, careful what you say. The dead are always watching us."

"The dead aren't watching anyone. They're minding their own business. The dead are shit."

"What do you mean they're shit?"

"All they do is fuck stuff up for the living."

"I'm afraid I can't agree there, compadre, I have the greatest respect for the departed."

"Except you never go to the cemetery."

"What do you mean I never go to the cemetery?"

"All right, then, when's the Day of the Dead?"

"OK, you got me, I go when I feel like it."

"Do you believe in ghosts?"

"I'm not sure, but I know there are experiences that make your hair stand on end."

"That's what I was coming to."

"You're thinking of Raulito Sánchez?"

"That's right. Before he died for real, he pretended to be dead at least twice. One time in a hooker's bar. Remember Doris Villalón? She spent a whole night with him in the cemetery, under the same blanket and, according to Doris, nothing happened all night."

"Except that Doris's hair turned white."

"It depends who you talk to."

"The fact is her hair went white in a single night, like Marie Antoinette's."

"What I know from a reliable source is that she was cold and they climbed into an empty niche; after that it's not so clear. According to one of Doris's friends, she tried to give Raulito a hand job, but he wasn't really up for it, and in the end he fell asleep."

"There was a man who never lost his cool."

"It happened later, when the dogs had stopped barking and Doris was climbing down from the niche; that's when the ghost appeared."

"So her hair went white because of a ghost?"

"That's what they said."

"Maybe it was just plaster dust from the cemetery."

"It's not easy to believe in ghosts."

"And meanwhile Raulito went on sleeping?"

"Without even having touched the poor woman."

"And what was his hair like the next morning?"

"Black as ever, but it couldn't be used to prove the point, because he'd upped and left."

"So the plaster dust might have had nothing to do with it."

"It might have been the scare she got."

"The scare she got at the police station."

"Or maybe her hair dye faded."

"Such are the mysteries of the human condition. In any case, Raulito never tried it with a girl."

"But he seemed like a real man."

"There are no men left in Chile, compadre."

"You're scaring me now. Careful how you drive. Don't get jumpy on me."

"I think it was a rabbit, I must have run over it."

"What do you mean there are no men left?"

"We killed them all."

"What do you mean we killed them? I haven't killed anyone in my life. And you were just doing your duty."

"My duty?"

"Duty, obligation, keeping the peace, it's our job, it's what we do. Or would you rather get paid for just sitting around?"

"I've never liked sitting around, I've always had ants in my pants, but that's exactly why I should have left."

"That just would have helped with the shortage of men in Chile."

"Don't start making fun of me, compadre, especially when I'm driving."

"You keep calm and watch where you're going. Anyway, what's Chile got to do with it?"

"Everything, and when I say everything . . ."

"OK, I see where you're going."

"Do you remember '73?"

"That's what I was thinking of."

"That's when we killed them all."

"Maybe you should go easy on the gas, at least while you explain what you mean."

"There's not a lot to explain. Plenty to cry over, but not to explain."

"But since it's a long trip, we might as well talk. Who did we kill in '73?"

"The real men we had in this country."

"No need to exaggerate, compadre. Anyway, we went first; don't forget we were prisoners too."

"But only for three days."

"But those were the first three days, and honestly I was scared shitless."

"Some were never released, like Inspector Tovar, Hick Tovar, remember him? He had guts, that guy."

"Didn't they drown him on Quiriquina Island?"

"That's what we told his widow, but the real story never came out."

"That's what I can't stand sometimes."

"No point getting cut up about it."

"The dead turn up in my dreams, and I get them mixed up with the ones who are neither dead nor alive."

"How do you mean neither dead nor alive?"

"I mean the people who've changed, who've grown up, like us, for instance."

"Now I get you—we're not children any more, if that's what you mean."

"And sometimes I feel like I'm never going to wake up, like I've gone and fucked it up for good."

"You just worry too much, compadre."

"And sometimes it makes me so angry I have to find someone to blame, you know what I'm like, those mornings when I turn up in a rotten mood, looking for someone to blame, but I can't find anyone, or I find the wrong person, which is worse, and then I go to pieces."

"Yeah, yeah, I know."

"And I blame Chile, and call it a country of faggots and killers."

"And why are the faggots to blame, can you tell me that?"

"Well, they're not, but everyone's fair game."

"I can't agree with you there; life's hard enough as it is."

"Then I think this country went to hell years ago, and the reason we're here, those of us who stayed, is to have nightmares, just because someone had to stay and face up to them."

"Watch it, there's a hill coming up. Don't look at me, I'm not arguing with you—watch where you're going."

"And that's when I think there are no men left in this country. It's like a revelation. There are no men left, just sleepwalkers."

"And what about the women?"

"You can be thick sometimes, compadre; I'm talking about the human condition, in general, and that includes women."

"I'm not sure I understand."

"Well, I was perfectly clear."

"So you're saying there are no men in Chile and no women who are men either."

"Not exactly, but almost."

"I think the women of Chile deserve a bit more respect."

"Who's disrespecting Chilean women?"

"You are, compadre, for a start."

"But how could I disrespect Chilean women? They're the only women I know."

"That's what you say, but it's lip-service, isn't it?"

"How come you're so touchy all of a sudden?"

"I'm not touchy."

"You know, I kind of feel like stopping and smashing your face in."

"We'll have to see about that."

"Jesus, what a beautiful night."

"Don't beautiful night me. What's the night got to do with anything?"

"It must be because of the full moon."

"Don't talk in riddles. I'm Chilean, remember, I don't believe in beating around the bush."

"That's where you're wrong. We're all Chileans here and all we ever do is beat around one great big fucking nightmare of a bush."

"You're a pessimist, that's what you are."

"What do you expect?"

"Even in the darkest hours there is a light that shines. I think it was Pezoa who said that."

"Pezoa Veliz."

"Even in the blackest moments a little hope remains."

"Hope has gone to shit."

"Hope is the only thing that doesn't go to shit."

"Pezoa Veliz. You know what I just remembered?"

"And how am I supposed to know that, compadre?"

"When we started in Criminal Investigations."

"At the station in Concepción?"

"At the station in Calle del Temple."

"All I remember about that station is the whores."

"I never fucked them."

"How can you say that, compadre?"

"I mean at the start, the first months; later on it was different, I started picking up bad habits."

"Anyway it was free, and when you fuck a whore and don't

pay, it's like you're not fucking a whore."

"A whore is always a whore."

"Sometimes I think you don't like women."

"What do you mean I don't like women?"

"It's the way you talk about them, with contempt."

"That's because, in my experience, when you get mixed up with whores it always goes sour."

"Come on, nothing in the world is sweeter."

"Yeah, sure, that's why we used to rape them."

"Are you talking about the station in Calle del Temple?"

"That's exactly what I'm talking about."

"Come on, we didn't rape them, that was an exchange of favors. It was a way of killing time. The next morning they went off perfectly happy after giving us a bit of relief. Don't you remember?"

"I remember lots of things."

"The interrogations were worse. I never volunteered."

"But you'd have done it if you'd been asked."

"I don't know what I would have done."

"You remember our classmate from high school who was a prisoner?"

"Of course I do, what was his name?"

"I was the one who realized he was there, though I still hadn't seen him myself. You'd seen him, but you didn't recognize him."

"We were twenty years old, compadre, and we hadn't seen the guy for at least five years. Arturo I think he was called. He didn't recognize me either."

"Yeah, Arturo. He left Chile when he was fifteen and came back when he was twenty."

"Bad timing, eh?"

"Good too, in a way, though, ending up at our station, of all the places he could have been taken . . ."

"Well, that's all ancient history now, we're all living in peace now."

"As soon as I saw his name on the list of political prisoners, I knew it was him. It's not a very common name."

"Watch where you're going; we can swap if you like."

"And the first thing I thought was, It's our old classmate Arturo, crazy Arturo, who went to Mexico when he was fifteen."

"Well, I reckon he was happy to find us there too."

"Of course he was happy! When you saw him he was incommunicado and the other prisoners had to feed him."

"He really was happy."

"It's like I'm seeing it now."

"But you weren't even there."

"No, but you told me. You said, You're Arturo Belano, aren't you, from Los Angeles, Bio-Bio. And he replied, Yes sir, I am."

"That's funny, I'd forgotten that."

"And then you said, Don't you remember me, Arturo? Don't you know who I am, asshole? And he looked at you as if he was thinking, Now it's my turn to get tortured or What does this son of a bitch want with me?"

"There was fear in his eyes, it's true."

"And he said, No, sir, I've got no idea, but he'd already started to look at you differently, peering through the fecal waters of the past, as the poet might say."

"There was fear in his eyes, that's all."

"And then you said, It's me, asshole, your classmate from high school in Los Angeles, five years ago. Don't you recognize me? Arancibia! And it was like he was making a huge effort, because five years is a long time and a lot of things had happened to him since he'd left Chile, plus what was happening now he'd come back, and he just couldn't place you, he could remember the faces of fifteen-year-olds, not twenty-year-olds, and anyway you were never one of his close friends."

"He was friends with everyone, but he used to hang out with the tough kids."

"You were never one of his close friends."

"I would've liked to be, though, I have to admit."

"And then he said, Arancibia, yeah, of course, Arancibia, and this is the funny bit, isn't it?"

"It depends. My partner wasn't amused at all."

"He grabbed you by the shoulders and gave you a thump in the chest that sent you flying back at least three yards."

"A yard and a half, just like the old days."

"And your partner jumped on him, of course, thinking the poor jerk had gone crazy."

"Or was trying to escape. We were so cocky back then we didn't take our guns off to do the roll call."

"In other words, your partner thought he was after your gun, so he jumped on him."

"And he would have laid into him, but I said he was a friend."

"And then you started slapping Belano on the back and said relax and told him what a good time we were having."

"I only told him about the whores; Jesus, we were green."

"You said, I get to screw a whore in the cells every night."

"No, I said we organized raids and then fucked until the sun came up, but only when we were on duty, of course."

"And he must have said, Fantastic, Arancibia, fantastic, glad to see you're keeping up the good work."

"Something like that; watch this curve."

"And you said to him, What are you doing here, Belano? Didn't you go to live in Mexico? And he told you he'd come back, and, of course, he said he was as innocent as the next man in the street."

"He asked me to do him a favor and let him make a phone call."

"And you let him use the phone."

"The same afternoon."

"And you told him about me."

"I said: Contreras is here, too. And he thought you were a prisoner."

"Shut up in a cell, screaming at three in the morning, like Chubby Martinazzo."

"Who was Martinazzo? I can't remember now."

"We had him there for a while. Belano would have heard him yelling every night, unless he was a heavy sleeper."

"But I said, No, compadre, Contreras is a detective too, and I whispered in his ear: But he's left-wing, don't go telling."

"That was bad; you shouldn't have said that."

"I wasn't going to hang you out to dry."

"And what did Belano say?"

"He looked like he didn't believe me. He looked like he didn't know who the hell Contreras was. He looked like he thought this fucking cop is going to take me to the slaughterhouse."

"Though he was a trusting sort of kid."

"Everyone's trusting at fifteen."

"I didn't even trust my own mother."

"What do you mean you didn't trust your own mother? You can't fool your mother."

"Exactly, that's why."

"And then I said to him: You'll see Contreras this morning, when they take you to the john, watch out for him, he'll give you a signal. And Belano said OK, but he wanted me to set up the phone call. That was all he cared about."

"So he could get someone to bring him food."

"Anyway, he was happy when I left him. Sometimes I think if we'd met in the street he mightn't even have said hello. It's a funny world."

"He wouldn't have recognized you. You weren't one of his friends at high school."

"Neither were you."

"But he did recognize me. When they took them out around eleven, all the political prisoners in single file, I went over near the corridor that led to the bathroom and gave him a nod. He was the youngest of the prisoners and he wasn't looking too good."

"But did he recognize you or not?"

"Of course he recognized me. We smiled at each other from a distance and then he believed the stuff you'd told him."

"And what had I told him? Come on, let's hear it."

"A whole heap of lies, as I found out when I went to see him."

"You went to see him?"

"That night, after they transferred the other prisoners. Belano was left all on his own, with hours to go before the new lot arrived, and his spirits were about as low as they could get."

"Even the toughest guys lose it inside."

"Well, he hadn't broken down, either, if that's what you mean."

"No, but nearly."

"Nearly, that's true. Also, a really weird thing happened to him. I think that's why I remembered him tonight."

"So what was this weird thing?"

"Well, it happened when he was incommunicado—you know how it was in that station: all it meant was that you starved, because you could send as many messages as you liked to people on the outside. Anyway, Belano was incommunicado, which meant that no one was bringing him any food, and he had no soap, no toothbrush, and no blanket to wrap himself in at night. And after a few days, of course, he was dirty, unshaven, his clothes stank, you know, the usual. The thing is, once a day we used to take all the prisoners to the bathroom, remember?"

"How could I forget?"

"And on the way to the bathroom there was a mirror, not in the bathroom itself, but in a corridor that ran between the bathroom and the gym where the political prisoners were kept, a tiny little mirror, near the records office, you remember, don't you?"

"I don't remember that, compadre."

"Well, there was this mirror, and all the political prisoners would look at themselves in it. We'd taken down the mirror in the showers, so no one would get any stupid ideas, and this was the only chance they got to see how well they'd shaved or how straight their part was, so they all had a look in it, especially when they'd been allowed to shave or the one day of the week when they got to take a shower."

"OK, I get you, and since Belano was incommunicado he couldn't even shave or take a shower or anything."

"Exactly, he didn't have a razor, or a towel, or soap, or clean clothes, and he never got to take a shower."

"But I can't remember him smelling really bad."

"Everyone stank. You could wash every day and still stink. You stank, too."

"You leave me out of it, compadre, and watch that embankment."

"Well, the thing is, when Belano was in the line with the prisoners, he always avoided looking at himself in the mirror. You see? He turned away. Whether he was going from the gym to the bathroom or from the bathroom back to the gym, when he got to the corridor with the mirror, he looked the other way."

"He was afraid to look at himself."

"Until one day, after finding out that his old schoolmates were there to get him out of that fix, he felt up to it. He'd been thinking about it all night and all morning. His luck had changed, so he decided to face the mirror and see how he looked."

"And what happened?"

"He didn't recognize himself."

"That's all?"

"That's all; he didn't recognize himself. He told me so the night I got a chance to talk with him. I really wasn't expecting him to come out with that. I'd gone to tell him not to get me wrong, I was really left-wing, I had nothing to do with all the shit that was happening, but he came out with this crap about the mirror and I didn't know what to say."

"And what did you say about me?"

"I didn't say anything at all. He did all the talking. He said it was a simple thing, it didn't come as a shock at all, if you see what I mean. He was in the line, on the way to the bathroom, and as he passed the mirror, he turned suddenly, looked at his face and saw someone else, but he wasn't frightened, he didn't start shaking or get hysterical. I guess you could say that by then, knowing we were there at the station, he had no reason to get hysterical. Anyway, he did what he needed to do in the bathroom, quietly, thinking about the person he'd seen, thinking it over, but not making a big deal of it. And when they went back to the gym, he looked in the mirror again, and sure enough, he said, it wasn't him, it was someone else, and I said to him, What are you saying, asshole? What do you mean someone else?"

"That's what I would have said, too. What *did* he mean?"

"He said, Someone else. And I said, Explain it to me. And he said, A different person, that's all."

"And then you thought he'd gone crazy."

"I don't know what I thought, but to be honest, I was scared."

"A Chilean? Scared?"

"You think that's so unusual?"

"Well, I wouldn't say it's usual for you."

"Whatever you say. I realized straightaway that he wasn't trying to kid me. I'd taken him to the little room beside the gym, and he started talking about the mirror and the way they had to file past it every morning, and suddenly I realized that all of it was true: him, me, our conversation. And since we weren't in the gym, and since he'd been a student at our grand old alma mater, it occurred to me that I could take him to the corridor where the mirror was and say, Take another look, with me here beside you this time, take a good calm look, and tell me if it isn't the same old crazy Belano you see."

"And did you say that?"

"Of course I did, but to be honest, the thought came a long

time before the words. As if an eternity had passed between the idea popping into my head and coming out in a comprehensible form. A little eternity, to make things worse. Because if it had been a big or just a regular eternity, I wouldn't have realized, if you follow me, but as it was, I did realize, and that intensified my fear."

"But you went ahead anyway."

"Of course I did; by then it was too late to turn back. I said, We're going to do a test; let's see if the same thing happens with me beside you, and he looked at me warily, but he said, All right, if you insist, like he was doing me a favor, when in fact I was the one doing him a favor, as usual."

"So you went to the mirror?"

"We went to the mirror. I was taking a big risk because you know what would have happened if they'd caught me walking around the station with a political prisoner at midnight. And to help him calm down and be as objective as possible, I offered him a smoke, so we stood there puffing away and it was only when we'd crushed the butts on the ground that we headed off toward the bathroom, and he was relaxed, I guess he was thinking it couldn't get any worse (which was bullshit, it could have been much, much worse), and I was kind of on edge, listening for the slightest noise, the sound of a door shutting, but I was careful not to let it show, and when we got to the mirror I said, Look at yourself, and he looked at himself, he stood in front of the mirror and looked at his face, he even ran a hand through his hair, which was really long, you know, the way people wore it in '73, and then he glanced aside, stepped away from the mirror and looked at the ground for a while."

"And?"

"That's what I said, And? Is it you or isn't it? And he looked into my eyes and said: It's someone else, compadre, that's all there is to it. I could feel something inside me like a muscle or a nerve, I don't know what it was, I swear, but it was saying: Smile, asshole, smile, and yet however much the muscle strained, I couldn't smile, the best I could do was twitch, a spasm jerked my cheek up, anyway, he noticed and stood there looking at me, and I ran a hand over my face and gulped, because I was afraid again."

"We're almost there."

"And then I had this idea. I said to him: Listen, I'm going to look in the mirror, and when I look at myself, you're going to look at me then you're going to look at my reflection, and you're going to realize it's the same, the problem is this filthy mirror and this filthy station and the bad lighting in this corridor. And he didn't say anything, but I took that as a yes—he could have objected—and I came up to the mirror and leaned forward with my eyes shut."

"You can see the lights already, compadre, we're just about there, take it easy."

"Are you playing deaf, or what? Didn't you hear me?"

"Of course I heard you. You had your eyes shut."

"I stood in front of the mirror with my eyes shut. And then I opened them. Maybe that's normal for you: standing in front of a mirror with your eyes shut."

"Nothing seems normal to me any more, compadre."

"Then I opened them, suddenly, I opened my eyes right up and looked at myself and saw someone staring back at me wide-eyed, like he was scared shitless, and behind him I saw a guy about twenty years old, but he looked at least ten years older, a skinny guy with a beard and bags under his eyes, looking at us over my shoulder, and to tell the truth, I couldn't be sure, I saw a swarm of faces, as if the mirror was broken, though I knew perfectly well it wasn't, and then Belano said, very softly, it was barely more than a whisper, he said: Hey, Contreras, is there some kind of room behind that wall?"

"The fuckhead! He'd seen too many movies!"

"And when I heard his voice it was like I woke up, but in reverse, and instead of coming back to this side, I'd come out on the other side, where even my own voice sounded strange. No, I said, as far as I know, behind it there's just the yard. The yard where the cells are? he asked me. Yes, I said, where the regular prisoners are. And then the son of a bitch said: Now I understand. And that completely flummoxed me, because, I mean, what was there to understand? And I said the first thing that came into my head: What the flying fuck do you understand now? But I said it softly, without raising my voice, so softly he didn't hear me, and I didn't have the strength to repeat the question. So I looked in the mirror again and saw two old classmates, a twenty-year-old cop with a loose tie, and a dirty-looking guy with long hair and a beard, all skin and bone, and I thought: Jesus, we really have fucked up, haven't we, Contreras. Then I put my hands on Belano's shoulders and led him back to the gym. When we came to the door a thought crossed my mind: I could take out my gun and shoot him right here; it would have been so easy, all I had to do was aim and put a bullet through his head, I've always been a good shot, even in the dark. Then I could have come up with any old explanation. But of course I didn't do it."

"Of course you didn't. We don't do that sort of thing, compadre."

"No, we don't do that sort of thing."

CELL MATES

We happened to be in prison in the same month of the same year, although the prisons were thousands of miles apart. Sofia was born in 1950 in Bilbao. She was dark, small and very pretty. In November 1973, while I was a prisoner in Chile, she was sent to jail in Aragon.

At the time she was getting her degree in science at the University of Zaragoza, biology or chemistry, one or the other, and she went to jail with almost all of her classmates. On the fourth or fifth night we slept together, as I was adopting a new position, she told me there was no point tiring myself out. I like variety, I said. If I fuck in the same position two nights in a row, I become impotent. Well, don't do it for my sake, she said. The room had a very high ceiling, and the walls were painted red, the color of a desert at sunset. She had painted them herself a few days after moving in. It looked awful. I've made love every way there is, she said. I don't believe you, I replied. Every way there is? That's right, she said, and I was at a loss for words (maybe I was embarrassed) but I believed her.

Later she told me, but this was quite a few days later, that she was losing her mind. She ate hardly anything, only instant mashed potatoes. Once I went into the kitchen and saw a plastic bag beside the refrigerator. It was a twenty-kilo bag of mashed potato flakes. Is that all you eat? I asked. She smiled and said yes—sometimes she ate other things, but mostly when she went out to a bar or a restaurant. At home it's simpler just to have mashed potatoes, she said. That way there's always something to eat. She didn't put milk in it, only water, and she didn't even wait for the water to boil. She mixed the flakes with warm water, she told me, because she hated milk. I never saw her consume any milk products; she said it was probably some kind of psychological problem that went back to her childhood, something to do with her mother. So when we were both in the apartment at night, she would have her mashed potatoes, and sometimes she would sit up late with me watching movies on TV. We hardly talked. She never argued. At the time there was a Communist living in the apartment; he was in his twenties, like us, and he and I used to get into long, pointless arguments, but she never joined in, although I knew she was more on my side than on his. One day the Communist told me Sofia was hot and he was planning to fuck her at the first opportunity. Go ahead, I said. Two or three nights later, while I was watching a Bardem movie, I heard him go out into the passage and knock discreetly on Sofia's door. They talked for a while and then the door closed and the Communist was in there for a good two hours.

Sofia had been married, though I didn't find out until much later. Her husband had been a student at the University of Zaragoza too, and gone to prison with the rest of them in November 1973. When they finished their degrees they moved to Barcelona and after a while they split up. He was called Emilio and they were still good friends. Did you make love every way there is with Emilio? No, but nearly, said Sofia. She also said she was losing her mind and it was a worry, especially if she was driving. The other night it happened in Diagonal, luckily there wasn't much traffic. Are you taking something? Valium. Lots and lots of Valium. Before we slept together, we went to the movies a couple of times. French movies, I think. One was about a woman pirate; she goes to this island where another woman pirate lives and they have a duel to the death with swords. The other one was set during World War Two; there was a guy who worked for the Germans and for the Resistance at the same time. After we started sleeping together we kept going to the movies and, strangely, I can remember the titles of the films we saw and the names of the directors, but nothing else about them. From the very first night Sofia made it perfectly clear that our relationship wasn't going to be serious. I'm in love with someone else, she said. Our Communist comrade? No, you don't know him; he's a teacher, like me. She didn't want to tell me his name just then. Sometimes she spent the night with him, but not very often, about once a fortnight. We made love every night. At first I tried to tire her out. We would start at eleven and keep going until four in the morning, but soon I realized there was no way of tiring out Sofia.

At the time I used to hang out with anarchists and radical feminists and the books I read were more or less influenced by the company I was keeping. There was one by an Italian feminist, Carla something, called *Let's Spit on Hegel*. One afternoon I lent it to Sofia. Read it, I said, I thought it was really good. (Maybe I said she would get a lot out of it.) The next day Sofia was in a very good mood; she gave me back the book and said that as science fiction it wasn't bad, but otherwise it sucked. Only an Italian woman could have written it, she declared. What have you got against Italian women? I asked. Did one abuse you when you were little or something? She said no, but if she was going to read that sort of thing, she preferred Valerie Solanas. I was surprised to learn that her favorite author was not a woman but an Englishman, David Cooper, one of R. D. Laing's associates. I ended up reading Valerie Solanas and David Cooper and even Laing (his sonnets). One of the things that impressed me most about Cooper was that during his time in Argentina (although I'm not sure now whether Cooper was ever really in Argentina, maybe I'm getting mixed up) he used hallucinogenic drugs to treat left-wing activists. These were people who were cracking up because they knew they could die at any moment, people who might not have the experience of growing old in real life, but they could have it with the drugs, and they got better. Sofia used drugs too, sometimes. She took LSD and amphetamines and Rohypnol, pills to speed up and pills to slow down and pills to steady her hands on the steering wheel. I rarely accepted the offer of a lift in her car. We didn't go out much, in fact. I went on with my life, she went on with hers, and at night, in her room or in mine, our bodies locked in a relentless struggle that lasted till daybreak and left us wrung out.

One afternoon Emilio came to see her and she introduced me to him. He was tall, he had a wonderful smile, and you could tell he was fond of Sofia. His girlfriend was called Nuria; she was Catalan and worked as a high school teacher, like Emilio and Sofia. You couldn't have imagined two women more different. Nuria was blonde, blue-eyed, tall and rather plump. Sofia had dark hair and brown eyes so dark they seemed black; she was short and slim as a marathon runner. In spite of everything they seemed to be good friends. As I found out later on, it was Emilio who had ended the marriage, although the separation had been amicable. Sometimes, when we'd been sitting there for a long time without talking, Nuria looked North American to me and Sofia looked Vietnamese. But Emilio just looked like Emilio, a chemistry or biology teacher from Aragon, who'd been an anti-Franco activist and a political prisoner, a decent sort of guy though not very interesting. One night Sofia told me about the man she was in love with. He was called Juan and he was a member of the Communist Party like our comrade. He worked in the same school as her, so they saw each other every day. He was married and had a son. So where do you do it? In my car, said Sofia, or his. We go out in our cars and follow each other through the streets of Barcelona, sometimes all the way to Tibidabo or Sant Cugat. Sometimes we just park in a dark street and he gets into my car or I get into his. Not long after she told me this, Sofia got sick and had to stay in bed. At that stage there were only three of us in the apartment: Sofia, the Communist and me. The Communist was only around at night so I had to look after Sofia and go to the pharmacy. One night she said we should go traveling. Where? I asked. Portugal, she said. I liked the idea, so one morning we set off for Portugal, hitchhiking. (I thought we would go in her car but Sofia was scared of driving.) It was a long and complicated trip. We stopped in Zaragoza, where Sofia still had her best friends, then at her sister's place in Madrid, then in Extremadura . . .

I got the feeling Sofia was visiting all her ex-lovers. I got the feeling she was saying goodbye to them one by one, but not in a calm or resigned sort of way. When we made love she seemed absent at first, as if it had nothing to do with her, but after a while she let herself go and ended up coming over and over. Then she started crying and I asked her why. Because I'm such an animal; even though I'm miles away, I can't help coming. Don't be so hard on yourself, I said, and we went on making love. Her face wet with tears was delicious to kiss. Her whole body burned and flexed like a red-hot piece of metal, but her tears were only lukewarm and, as they ran down her neck, as I spread them on her nipples, they turned ice-cold. A month later we were back in Barcelona. Sofia hardly ate a thing all day. She went back to her diet of instant mashed potatoes and decided not to leave the apartment. One night I came home and found her with a girl I didn't know; another time it was Emilio and Nuria, who looked at me as if I were to blame for the state she was in. I felt bad but said nothing and shut myself in my room. I tried to read, but I could hear them. Shocked exclamations, reprimands, advice. Sofia didn't say a thing. A week later she was given four months' sick leave. The government doctor was an old friend from Zaragoza. I thought we'd be able to spend more time together, but little by little we drifted apart. Some nights she didn't come home. I remember staying up very late, watching TV and waiting for her. Sometimes the Communist kept me company. I had nothing to do, so I set about tidying up the apartment: sweeping, mopping, dusting. The Communist was very impressed, but one day he had to go too and I was left all on my own.

By then Sofia had become a ghost; she appeared without a sound, shut herself in her room or the bathroom and disappeared again after a few hours. One night we ran into each other on the stairs, I was going up and she was coming down, and the only thing I could think of asking was if she had a new lover. I regretted it straightaway, but it was too late. I can't remember what she said. In the good old days, five of us had lived in that huge apartment; now it was just me and the mice. Sometimes I imagined Sofia in a prison cell in Zaragoza, back in November 1973, and me, in the southern hemisphere, locked up too, for a few decisive days, and though I realized that this fact or coincidence had to be significant, I couldn't work out what it meant. I've never been any good at analogies. One night, when I came home, I found a note saying goodbye and some money on the kitchen table. At first I went on living as if Sofia was still there. I can't remember exactly how long I waited for her. I think the electricity got cut off. After that I moved to another apartment.

It was a long time before I saw her again. She was walking down Las Ramblas, looking lost. We stood there, the cold seeping into our bones, talking about things that meant nothing to her or to me. Walk me home, she said. She was living near El Borne, in a building that was falling down it was so old. The staircase was narrow and creaked with every step we took. We climbed up to the door of her apartment, on the top floor. To my surprise, she didn't let me in. I should have asked her what was going on, but I left without saying anything; if that's what she wanted, it was up to her.

A week later I went back to her apartment. The bell wasn't working and I had to knock several times. I thought there was no one there. Then I thought there was no one *living* there. Just as I was about to go, the door opened. It was Sofia. The apartment was dark and the light on the landing went off automatically after twenty seconds. At first, because of the darkness, I didn't realize she was naked. You're going to freeze, I said when the landing light came on again and showed her standing there, very straight, thinner than before. Her stomach and legs, which I had kissed so many times, looked terribly helpless, and instead of feeling drawn toward her, I was chilled at the sight, as if I were the one without clothes. Can I come in? Sofia shook her head. I assumed her nakedness meant that she was not alone. I said as much, and smiling stupidly, assured her that I didn't mean to be indiscreet. I was about to go back down the stairs when she said she was alone. I stopped and looked at her, more carefully this time, trying to read her expression, but her face was indecipherable. I also looked over her shoulder. Nothing had stirred in the utter silence and darkness of the apartment, but my instinct told me that someone was hiding there, listening to us, waiting. Are you feeling all right? Fine, she said very quietly. Have you taken something? No, nothing, I haven't taken any drugs, she whispered. Are you going to let me in? Can I make you some tea? No, said Sofia. Since I was asking questions, I thought I might as well try one more: Why won't you let me see your apartment, Sofia? Her answer surprised me. My boyfriend will be back soon and he doesn't like it if there's anyone here with me, especially a man. I didn't know whether to be angry or treat it as a joke. Sounds like this boyfriend of yours is a vampire, I said. Sofia smiled for the first time, although it was a weak, distant smile. I've told him about you, she said. He'd recognize you. And what would he do? Hit me? No, he'd just get angry, she said. And kick me out? (Now I was starting to get indignant. For a moment I hoped he did turn up, this boyfriend Sofia was waiting for, naked in the dark, just to see what would happen, what he would do.) He wouldn't kick you out, she said. He'd just get angry; he wouldn't talk to you and after you went he'd hardly say a word to me. You've lost it, haven't you, I spluttered, I don't know if you realize what you're saying, they've done something to you, it's like you're a different person. I'm the same as ever; you're the idiot who can't see what's going on. Sofia, Sofia, what's happened to you? You never used to be like this. Get out, just go, she said—What would you know about me?

More than a year went by before I heard any news of Sofia. One afternoon, coming out of the cinema, I ran into Nuria. We recognized each other, started talking about the movie and decided to go and have coffee. It wasn't long before we got on to Sofia. How long since you saw her? she asked me. A long time, I told her, but I also said that some mornings, when I woke up, I felt as if I had just seen her. Like you've been dreaming about her? No, I said, like I'd spent the night with her. That's weird. Something like that used to happen to Emilio too. Until she tried to kill him. Then he stopped having the nightmares.

She told me the story. It was simple. It was incomprehensible.

Six or seven months earlier, Sofia had rung up Emilio. According to what he later told Nuria, Sofia mentioned monsters, conspiracies and murders: she said the only thing that scared her more than a mad person was someone who deliberately drove others to madness. Then she arranged for him to come to her apartment, the one I'd been to a couple of times. The next day Emilio arrived exactly on time. The dark or poorly lit staircase, the bell that didn't work, the knocking at the door: up to that point it was all familiar and predictable. Sofia opened the door. She wasn't naked. She invited him in. Emilio had never been in the apartment before. The living room, according to Nuria, was pokey, but it was also in a terrible state, with filth dripping down the walls and dirty plates piled on the table. At first Emilio couldn't see a thing, the light was so dim in the room. Then he made out a man sitting in an armchair, and greeted him. The man didn't react. Sit down, said Sofia, we need to talk. Emilio sat down. A little voice inside him was saying over and over, This is not good, but he ignored it. He thought Sofia was going to ask him for a loan. Again. Although probably not with that man in the room. Sofia never asked for money in the presence of a third party, so Emilio sat down and waited.

Then Sofia said: There are one or two things about life that my husband would like to explain to you. For a moment Emilio thought that when she said "my husband" she meant him. He thought she wanted him to say something to her new boyfriend. He smiled. He started saying there was really nothing to explain; every experience is unique . . . Suddenly Emilio understood that he was the "you" and the "husband" was the other man, and that something bad was about to happen, something very bad. As he tried to get to his feet, Sofia threw herself at him. What followed was rather comical. Sofia held or tried to hold Emilio's legs while her new boyfriend made a sincere but clumsy attempt to strangle him. Sofia, however, was small and so was the nameless man (somehow, in the midst of the struggle, Emilio had time and presence of mind enough to notice the resemblance between them—they were like twins) and the fight, or the caricature thereof, was soon over. Maybe it was fear that gave Emilio a taste for revenge: as soon as he got Sofia's boyfriend down on the ground he started kicking him and kept going until he was tired. He must have broken a few ribs, said Nuria, you know what Emilio's like (I didn't, but nodded all the same). Then he turned his attention to Sofia who was ineffectually trying to hold him back from behind and hitting him, although he could hardly feel it. He gave her three slaps (it was the first time he had ever laid a hand on her, according to Nuria) and left. Since then they had heard nothing about her, though Nuria still got scared at night, especially when she was coming home from work.

I'm telling you all this in case you ever feel like visiting Sofia, said Nuria. No, I said, I haven't seen her for ages and I don't have any plans to drop in on her. Then we talked about other things for a little while and said good-bye. Two days later, without really knowing what prompted me to do it, I went round to Sofia's apartment.

She opened the door. She was thinner than ever. At first she didn't recognize me. Do I look that different, Sofia? I muttered. Oh, it's you, she said. Then she sneezed and took a step back. Perhaps mistakenly, I interpreted this as an invitation to go in. She didn't stop me.

The room in which they had set up the ambush was poorly lit (the only window gave onto a gloomy, narrow air shaft) but it didn't seem dirty. In fact the first thing that struck me was how clean it was. Sofia didn't seem dirty either. I sat down in an armchair, maybe the one Emilio had sat in on the day of the ambush, and lit a cigarette. Sofia was still standing, looking at me as if she wasn't quite sure who I was. She was wearing a long, narrow skirt, more suitable for summer, a light top and sandals. She had thick socks on and for a moment I thought they were mine, but no, they couldn't have been. I asked her how she was. She didn't answer. I asked her if she was alone, if she had something to drink and how life was treating her. She just stood there so I got up and went into the kitchen. It was clean and dark; the refrigerator was empty. I looked in the cupboards. Not even a miserable tin of peas. I turned on the tap; at least she had running water, but I didn't dare drink it. I went back to the living room. Sofia was still standing quietly in the same place, expectantly or absently, I couldn't tell, in any case just like a statue. I felt a gust of cold air and thought the front door must have been open. I went to check, but no. Sofia had shut it after I came in. That was something, at least, I thought.

What happened next is confused, or perhaps that's how I prefer to remember it. I was looking at Sofia's face—was she sad or pensive or simply ill?—I was looking at her profile and I knew that if I didn't do something I was going to start crying, so I went and hugged her from behind. I remember the passage that led to the bedroom and another room, the way it narrowed. We made love slowly, desperately, like in the old days. It was cold. I didn't get undressed. But Sofia took off all her clothes. Now you're cold as ice, I thought, cold as ice and on your own.

The next day I came back to see her again. This time I stayed much longer. We talked about when we used to live together and the TV shows we used to watch till the early hours of the morning. She asked me if I had a TV in my new apartment. I said no. I miss it, she said, especially the late-night shows. The good thing about not having a TV is you have more time to read, I said. I don't read any more, she said. Not at all? Not at all—have a look, there's not a single book here. Like a sleepwalker I got up and went all round the apartment, looking in every corner, as if I had all the time in the world. I saw many things, but no books. One of the rooms was locked and I couldn't go in. I came back with an empty feeling in my chest and dropped into Emilio's armchair. Up till then I hadn't asked about her boyfriend. So I did. Sofia looked at me and smiled for the first time, I think, since we'd met again. It was a brief but perfect smile. He's gone away, she said, and he's never coming back. Then we got dressed and went out to eat at a pizzeria.

CLARA

She had big breasts, slim legs and blue eyes. That's how I like to remember her. I don't know why I fell madly in love with her, but I did, and for a start, I mean for the first days, the first hours, it all went fine; then Clara returned to the city where she lived in the south of Spain (she'd been on vacation in Barcelona), and everything started to fall apart.

One night I dreamed of an angel: I walked into a huge, empty bar and saw him sitting in a corner with his elbows on the table and a cup of milky coffee in front of him. She's the love of your life, he said, looking up at me, and the force of his gaze, the fire in his eyes, threw me right across the room. I started shouting, Waiter, waiter, then opened my eyes, and escaped from that miserable dream. Other nights I didn't dream of anyone, but woke up in tears. Meanwhile, Clara and I were writing to each other. Her letters were brief. Hi, how are you, it's raining, I love you, bye. At first those letters scared me. It's all over, I thought. Nevertheless, after inspecting them more carefully, I reached the conclusion that her epistolary concision was motivated by a desire to avoid grammatical errors. Clara was proud. She couldn't write well, and she didn't want to let it show, even if it meant hurting me by seeming cold.

She was eighteen at the time. She had left high school and was studying music at a private academy and drawing with a retired landscape painter, but she wasn't all that interested in music, or in painting, really: she liked it, but couldn't get passionate about it. One day I received a letter informing me, in her usual terse fashion, that she was going to take part in a beauty contest. My response, which filled three double-sided pages, was an extravagant paean to her calm beauty, the sweetness of her eyes, the perfection of her figure, etc. The letter was a triumph of bad taste, and when I had finished it, I wondered whether or not I should send it, but in the end I did.

A few weeks went by before I heard from her. I could have called, but I didn't want to intrude and also at the time I was broke. Clara came second in the contest and was depressed for a week. Surprisingly, she sent me a telegram, which read: SECOND PLACE. STOP. GOT YOUR LETTER. STOP. COME AND SEE ME. The stops were written out.

A week later, I took a train bound for the city where she lived, the first one leaving that day. Before that, of course—I mean after the telegram—we had spoken on the phone, and I had heard the story of the beauty contest a number of times. It had made a big impact on Clara, apparently. So I packed my bags and, as soon as I could, got on a train, and very early the next morning, there I was, in that unfamiliar city. I arrived at Clara's apartment at nine-thirty, after having a coffee at the station and smoking a few cigarettes to kill some time. A fat woman with messy hair opened the door, and when I said I had come to see Clara, she looked at me as if I were a lamb on its way to the slaughterhouse. For a few minutes (which seemed extraordinarily long at the time, and thinking the whole thing over, later on, I realized that, in fact, they were), I sat in the living room and waited for her, a living room that seemed welcoming, for no special reason, overly cluttered, but welcoming and full of light. When Clara made her entrance it was like the apparition of a goddess. I know it was a stupid thing to think—and is a stupid thing to say—but that's how it was.

The following days were pleasant and unpleasant. We saw a lot of movies, almost one a day; we made love (I was the first guy Clara had slept with, which seemed incidental or anecdotal, but in the end it would cost me dearly); we walked around; I met Clara's friends; we went to two horrific parties; and I asked her to come and live with me in Barcelona. Of course, at that stage, I knew what her answer would be. A month later, I took a night train back to Barcelona; I remember it was a terrible trip.

Soon after that, Clara explained in a letter, the longest one she ever sent me, why she couldn't go on: I was putting her under intolerable pressure (by suggesting that we live together); it was all over. After that we talked three or four times on the phone. I think I also wrote her a letter containing insults and declarations of love. Once when I was traveling to Morocco, I called her from the hotel where I was staying, in Algeciras, and that time we were able to have a civilized conversation. At least she thought it was civilized. Or I did.

Years later Clara told me about the parts of her life I had missed out on. And then, years after that, both she and some of her friends told me her life story all over again, starting from the beginning or from the point where we split up—it didn't make any difference to them (I was a very minor character, after all), or to me, really, although that wasn't so easy to admit. Predictably, not long after the end of our engagement

(I know "engagement" is hyperbolic, but it's the best word I can find), Clara got married, and the lucky man was, logically enough, one of the friends I met on my first trip to her city.

But before that, she had psychological problems: she used to dream about rats; at night she would hear them in her bedroom, and for months, the months leading up to her marriage, she had to sleep on the sofa in the living room. I'm guessing those damn rats disappeared after the wedding.

So. Clara got married. And the husband, Clara's dear husband, surprised everyone, even her. After one or two years, I'm not sure exactly—Clara told me, but I've forgotten—they split up. It wasn't an amicable separation. The guy shouted, Clara shouted, she slapped him, he responded with a punch that dislocated her jaw. Sometimes, when I'm alone and can't get to sleep, but don't feel up to switching on the light, I think of Clara, who came in second in that beauty contest, with her jaw hanging out of joint, unable to get it back into place on her own, driving to the nearest hospital with one hand on the wheel, and the other supporting her jawbone. I'd like to find it funny, but I can't.

What I do find funny is her wedding night. The day before, she'd had an operation, for hemorrhoids, so I guess she was still a bit groggy. Or maybe not. I never asked her if she was able to make love with her husband. I think they'd done it before the operation. Anyway, what does it matter? All these details say more about me than they do about her.

In any case, Clara split up with her husband a year or two after the wedding, and started studying. She hadn't finished high school, so she couldn't go to a university, but she tried everything else: photography, painting (I don't know why, but she always thought she could be a good painter), music, typing, computers, all those one-year diploma courses supposedly leading to job opportunities that desperate young people keep jumping at or falling for. And although Clara was happy to have escaped from a husband who beat her, deep down she was desperate.

The rats came back, and the depression, and the mysterious illnesses. For two or three years she was treated for an ulcer, until the doctors finally realized that there was nothing wrong, at least not in her stomach. Around that time she met Luis, an executive; they became lovers, and he convinced her to study something related to business administration. According to Clara's friends, she had at last found the love of her life. Before long, they were living together; Clara got a job in an office, a legal firm or some kind of agency—a really fun job, Clara said, without a hint of irony—and her life seemed to be on track, for good this time. Luis was a sensitive guy (he never hit her), and cultured (he was, I believe, one of the two million Spaniards who bought the complete works of Mozart in installments), and patient too (he listened, he listened to her every night and on the weekends). And although Clara didn't have much to say for herself, she never got tired of saying it. She wasn't fretting over the beauty contest any more, although she did bring it up from time to time; now it was all about her periods of depression, her mental instability, the pictures she had wanted to paint but hadn't.

I don't know why they didn't have children, maybe they didn't have time, although, according to Clara, Luis was crazy about kids. But she wasn't ready. She used her time to study, and listen to music (Mozart, but then other composers too), and take photographs, which she never showed anyone. In her own obscure and futile way, she tried to defend her freedom, tried to learn.

At the age of thirty-one, she slept with a guy from the office. It was just something that happened, not a big deal, at least for the two of them, but Clara made the mistake of telling Luis. The fight was appalling. Luis smashed a chair or a painting he had bought himself, got drunk, and didn't talk to her for a month. According to Clara, from that day on, nothing was the same, in spite of the reconciliation, in spite of their trip to a town on the coast, a rather sad and dull trip, as it turned out.

At thirty-two, her sex life was almost nonexistent. Shortly before she turned thirty-three, Luis told her that he loved her, he respected her, he would never forget her, but for some months he had been seeing someone from work, who was divorced and had children, a nice, understanding woman, and he was planning to go and live with her.

On the surface, Clara took the break-up pretty well (it was the first time someone had left her). But a few months later she lapsed into depression again and had to take some time off work and undergo psychiatric treatment, which didn't help much. The medication suppressed her libido, although she did make some willful but unsatisfactory attempts to sleep with other men, including me. She started talking about the rats again; they wouldn't leave her alone. When she got nervous she had to go to the bathroom constantly (the first night we slept together, she must have gotten up to pee ten times). She talked about herself in the third person; in fact, she once told me that there were three Claras in her soul: a little girl, an old crone enslaved by her family, and a young woman, the real Clara, who wanted to get out of that city forever, and paint, and take photos, and travel, and live. For the first few days after we got back together, I feared for her life. Sometimes I wouldn't even go out shopping because I was scared of coming back and finding her dead, but as the days went by my fears gradually faded away and I realized (or perhaps conveniently convinced myself) that Clara wasn't going to take her own life; she wasn't going to throw herself off the balcony of her apartment—she wasn't going to do anything.

Soon after that, I left, but this time I decided to call her every so often, and stay in touch with one of her friends, who could fill me in (if only now and then). That's how I came to know a few things it might have been easier not to have known, stories that did nothing for my peace of mind, the kind of news an egotist should always take care to avoid. Clara went back to work (the new pills she was taking had done wonders for her outlook), but before long she was transferred to a branch in another Andalusian city—though not very far away—maybe to pay her back for such a long absence. She moved, started going to the gym (at thirty-four she was no longer the beauty I had known at seventeen), and made new friends. That's how she met Paco, who was divorced, like her.

Before long, they were married. At first, Paco would tell anyone prepared to listen what he thought of Clara's photos and paintings. And Clara thought that Paco was intelligent and had good taste. As time went by, however, Paco lost interest in Clara's esthetic efforts and wanted to have a child. Clara was thirty-five and at first she wasn't keen on the idea, but she gave in, and they had a child. According to Clara, the child satisfied all her yearnings—that was the word she used. According to her friends, she was getting steadily worse, whatever that meant.

On one occasion, for reasons irrelevant to this story, I had to spend a night in the city where Clara was living. I called her from the hotel, told her where I was, and we arranged to meet the following day. I would have preferred to see her that night, but after our previous encounter Clara regarded me, and perhaps with good reason, as a kind of enemy, so I didn't insist.

She was almost unrecognizable. She had put on weight and although she was wearing makeup her face looked worn, not so much by time as by frustration, which surprised me, since I'd never really thought that Clara aspired to anything. And if you don't aspire to anything, how can you be frustrated? Her smile had also undergone a transformation. Before, it had been warm and slightly dumb, the smile of a young lady from a provincial capital, but it had become a mean, hurtful smile, and it was easy to read the resentment, rage and envy behind it. We kissed each other on the cheeks like a pair of idiots and then sat down; for a while we didn't know what to say. I was the one who broke the silence. I asked about her son; she told me he was at day care, and then she asked me about mine. He's fine, I said. We both realized that unless we did something, that meeting was going to become unbearably sad. How do I look? asked Clara. It was as if she were asking me to slap her. Same as ever, I replied automatically. I remember we had a coffee, then went for a walk along an avenue lined with plane trees, which led directly to the station. My train was about to leave. We said good-bye at the door of the station, and that was the last time I saw her.

We did, however, talk on the phone before she died. I used to call her every three or four months. I had learned from experience not to touch on personal or intimate matters (a bit like sticking to sports when chatting with strangers in bars), so we talked about her family, which, in those conversations, remained as abstract as a cubist poem, or her son's school, or her job at the office; she was still at the same place, and over the years she had got to know about all her colleagues and their lives, and all the problems the executives were having—those secrets gave her an intense and perhaps excessive pleasure. On one occasion I tried to get her to say something about her husband, but at that point Clara clammed up. You deserve the best, I told her once. That's strange, replied Clara. What's strange? I asked. It's strange that you should say that—you, of all people, said Clara. I quickly tried to change the subject, claimed I was running out of coins (I've never had a phone of my own, and never will; I always called from a phone booth), hurriedly said good-bye and hung up. I realized I couldn't face another argument with Clara; I couldn't listen to her working up another one of her endless justifications.

One night, not long ago, she told me she had cancer. Her voice was as cold as ever, the voice in which, years before, she had announced that she was going to compete in a beauty contest, the voice in which she recounted her life with the detachment of a bad storyteller, putting exclamation marks in all the wrong places, and passing over what she should have gone into, the parts where she should have cut to the quick. I remember asking her if she had already been to see a doctor, as if she had diagnosed the cancer herself (or with Paco's help). Of course, she said. At the other end of the line I heard something like a croak. She was laughing. We talked briefly about our children, and then (she must have been feeling lonely or bored) she asked me to tell her something about my life. I made something up on the spot and said I'd call her back the following week. That night I slept very badly. I had one nightmare after another, and woke up suddenly, shouting, convinced that Clara had lied to me: she didn't have cancer; something was happening to her, for sure, the way things had been happening for the last twenty years, little, fucked-up things, all full of shit and smiles, but she didn't have cancer. It was five in the morning. I got up and walked to the Paseo Marítimo, with the wind at my back, which was strange because the wind usually blows in from the sea, and hardly ever from the opposite direction. I didn't stop until I got to the phone booth next to one of the biggest cafés on the Paseo. The terrace was empty, the chairs were chained to the tables, but a little way off, right near the seaside, a homeless guy was sleeping on a bench, with his knees drawn up, and every now and then he shuddered, as if he were having nightmares.

My address book only contained one other number in Clara's city. I called it. After a long time, a woman's voice answered. I said who I was, but suddenly found I couldn't say anything more. I thought she'd hang up, but I heard the click of a lighter and smoke rushing in through lips. Are you still there? asked the woman. Yes, I said. Have you talked to Clara? Yes, I said. Did she tell you she had cancer? Yes, I said. Well, it's true.

All the years since I had met Clara suddenly came tumbling down on top of me, everything my life had been, most of it nothing to do with her. I don't know what else the woman said at the other end of the line, hundreds of miles away; I think I began to cry in spite of myself, like in the poem by Rubén Darío. I fumbled in my pockets for cigarettes, listened to fragments of stories: doctors, operations, mastectomies, discussions, different points of view, deliberations, the activities of a Clara I couldn't know or touch or help, not now. A Clara who could never save me now.

When I hung up, the homeless guy was standing about five feet away. I hadn't heard him approaching. He was very tall, too warmly dressed for the season, and he was staring at me, as if he were near-sighted or worried I might make a sudden move. I was so sad I didn't even get a fright, although afterwards, walking back through the twisting streets of the town center, I realized that, seeing him, I had forgotten Clara for an instant, and that was just the start.

We talked on the phone quite often after that. Some weeks I called her twice a day: they were short, stupid conversations, and there was no way to say what I really wanted to say, so I talked about anything, the first thing that came into my head, some nonsense I hoped would make her smile. Once I got nostalgic and tried to summon up days gone by, but Clara put on her icy armor, and I soon got the message and gave up on nostalgia. As the date of the operation approached, my calls became more frequent. Once I talked with her son. Another time with Paco. They both seemed well, they sounded well, at least not as nervous as me. Although I'm probably wrong about that. Certainly wrong, in fact. Everyone's worried about me, said Clara one afternoon. I thought she meant her husband and her son, but "everyone" included many more people, many more than I could imagine, everyone. The day before she was to go into the hospital, I called her in the afternoon. Paco answered. Clara wasn't there. No one had seen her or heard from her in two days. From Paco's tone of voice I sensed that he suspected she might be with me. I told him straight up: She's not here, but that night I hoped with all my heart that she would come to my place. I waited for her with the lights on, and finally fell asleep on the sofa, and dreamed of a very beautiful woman who was not Clara: a tall, slim woman, with small breasts, long legs, and deep brown eyes, who was not and never would be Clara, a woman whose presence obliterated Clara, reduced her to a poor, lost, trembling forty-something-year-old.

She didn't come to my apartment.

The next day I called Paco. And two days after that I phoned again. There was still no sign of Clara. The third time I called Paco, he talked about his son and complained about Clara's behavior. Every night I wonder where she could be, he said. From his voice and the turn the conversation was taking, I could tell that what he needed from me, or someone, anyone, was friendship. But I was in no condition to provide him with that solace.

JOANNA SILVESTRI

for Paula Massot

Here I am, Joanna Silvestri, thirty-seven years of age, profession: porn star, on my back in the Clinique Les Trapèzes in Nîmes, watching the afternoons go by, listening to the stories of a Chilean detective. Who is this man looking for? A ghost? I know a lot about ghosts, I told him the second afternoon, the last time he came to see me, and he smiled like an old rat, like an old rat agreeing listlessly, like an improbably polite old rat. Anyway, thank you for the flowers and the magazines, but I can barely remember the person you're looking for, I told him. Don't rack your brains, he said, I've got plenty of time. When a man says he has plenty of time, he's already snared (so how much time he has is irrelevant), and you can do whatever you like with him. But of course that isn't true. Sometimes I get to thinking about the men who've lain at my feet, and I shut my eyes and when I open them again the walls of the room are painted other colors, not the bone white I see every day, but streaky vermilion, nauseous blue, like the daubs of that awful painter, Attilio Corsini. Awful paintings I'd rather not remember, but I do, and that memory flushes out others, like an enema, other memories with a sepia tone to them, which set the afternoons wavering slightly and are hard to bear at first but in the end they can even be fun. I haven't had that many men at my feet, actually: two or three, and it didn't last, they're all behind me now—that's just the way of the world. That's what I was thinking, and I would have liked to share it with him, even though I didn't know him at all, but I didn't say any of this to the Chilean detective. And as if to make up for that lack of generosity, I called him Detective, I might have said something about solitude and intelligence, and although he hastened to say, I'm not a detective, Madame Silvestri, I could tell that he was glad I'd said it; I was looking into his eyes when I spoke, and although he didn't seem to turn a hair, I noticed the fluttering, as if a bird had flown through his head. One thing stood in for the other: I didn't say what I was thinking, but I said something that I knew he would like. I said something that I knew would bring back pleasant memories. As if someone, preferably a stranger, were to speak to me now about the Civitavecchia Adult Film Festival or the Berlin Erotic Film Fair, or the Barcelona Exhibition of Pornographic Cinema and Video, and mention my triumphs, my real and imaginary triumphs, or about 1990—the best year of my life—when I went to Los Angeles, almost under duress, on a Milan-LA flight that I thought would be exhausting but in fact it went by like a dream, like the dream I had on the plane (it must have been somewhere over the Atlantic): I dreamed that we were heading for Los Angeles but going via Asia, with stops in Turkey, India and China, and from the window—I don't know why the plane was flying so low, but at no point were we, the passengers, at risk—I could see trains stretching away in vast caravans, a mad but precisely orchestrated railway mobilization, like an enormous clockwork mechanism spread out over the region, not a part of the world that I know (except for a trip to India in 1987, which is better forgotten), and there were people embarking and disembarking and goods being loaded and unloaded, all of it clearly visible, as if I were looking at one of those animations that economists use to explain how things work, their origins and destinations, their movement and inertia. And when I arrived in Los Angeles, Robbie Pantoliano, Adolfo Pantoliano's brother, was waiting for me at the airport, and as soon as I saw Robbie I could tell he was a gentleman, quite the opposite of his brother Adolfo (may he rest in peace or do his time in purgatory, I wouldn't wish hell on anyone), and outside there was a limousine waiting for me, the kind you only see in Los Angeles, not even in New York, only in Beverly Hills or Orange County, and we went to the place they'd rented for me, a unit by the beach, it was small but sweet, and Robbie and his secretary Ronnie stayed to help me unpack my bags (though I said really I'd prefer to do it on my own) and explain how everything worked in the unit, as if I didn't know what a microwave oven was—Americans are like that sometimes, so nice they end up being rude—and then they put on a video so I could see the actors I'd be working with: Shane Bogart, who I knew already from a movie I'd done with Robbie's brother; Bull Edwards, I didn't know him; Darth Krecick, the name rang a bell; Jennifer Pullman, another stranger to me, and so on, three or four others, and then Robbie and Ronnie left me on my own, and I double locked the doors as they had insisted I must, and then I took a bath, wrapped myself in a black bathrobe and looked for an old movie on TV, something to relax me completely, and at some point I fell asleep there on the sofa. The next day we started shooting. It was all so different from the way I remembered it. In two weeks we made four movies in all, with more or less the same team, and working for Robbie Pantoliano was like playing and working at the same time; it was like one of those day trips that office workers and bureaucrats organize in Italy, especially in Rome: once a year they all go out to the country for a meal and leave the office and its worries behind, but this was better, the sun was better, and the apartments and the sea, and catching up with the girls I'd known before, and the atmosphere on the set: debauched but fresh, the way it should be, and I think it came up when I was talking with Shane Bogart and one of the girls, the way things had changed, and naturally, for a start, I put it down to the death of Adolfo Pantoliano, who was a thug and a crook of the worst kind, a guy who had no respect, not even for his own long-suffering whores; when a bastard like that disappears, you're bound to notice the difference, but Shane Bogart said no, it wasn't that; Pantoliano's death, which had come as a relief, even to his own brother, was just a detail in the bigger picture, the industry was undergoing major changes, he said, because of a combination of apparently unrelated factors: money, new players coming in from other sectors, the disease, the demand for a product that would be different but not too different; then they started talking about money and the way a lot of porn stars were crossing over to the regular movie industry at the time, but I wasn't listening, I was thinking back to what they'd said about the disease, and remembering Jack Holmes, who'd been California's number one porn star just a few years before, and when we finished up that day I said to Robbie and Ronnie that I'd like to find out how Jack Holmes was doing, and asked them if they had his number, if he was still living in Los Angeles. And although Robbie and Ronnie thought it was a crazy idea at first, eventually they gave me Jack's phone number and told me to call him if that's what I wanted to do, but not to expect him to be coherent, or to hear the voice I remembered from the old days. That night I had dinner with Robbie and Ronnie and Sharon Grove, who had crossed over to horror and even claimed that she was going to be in the next Carpenter or Clive Barker film, which annoyed Ronnie, hearing those two lumped together, because, for him, only a handful of directors came anywhere near Carpenter, and Danny Lo Bello was there at the dinner too—I had a thing with him when we were working together in Milan—and Patricia Page, his eighteen-year-old wife, who only worked in Danny's movies, with a contract stipulating that only her husband was allowed to penetrate her, with the other guys she just sucked their cocks, and even that she did reluctantly; the directors weren't too happy with her, and according to Robbie sooner or later she'd either have to change careers or her and Danny would have to come up with some really sensational numbers. So there I was, having dinner in one of the best restaurants in Venice Beach, looking out at the sea, exhausted after a hard day's work, not paying much attention to the lively conversation at our table—I was miles away, thinking of Jack Holmes, remembering the way he looked: a very tall, thin guy with a long nose and long, hairy arms like the arms of an ape, but what kind of ape would Jack have been? An ape in captivity, no doubt about that, a melancholy ape or maybe the ape of melancholy, which might seem like the same thing but it's not, and when dinner was over, it wasn't too late for me to call Jack at home—people have dinner early in California, sometimes they finish before it gets dark—I couldn't wait any longer, I don't know what came over me, I asked Robbie for his cell phone and took myself off to a sort of jetty, all made of wood, a kind of miniature wooden pier exclusively for tourists, with waves breaking under it, long, low, almost foamless waves that took an eternity to dissipate, and I phoned Jack Holmes. I honestly didn't expect him to answer. At first I didn't recognize his voice, it was like Robbie said, and he didn't recognize mine either. It's me, I said, Joanna Silvestri, I'm in Los Angeles. Jack was quiet for a long time and all of a sudden I realized I was shaking, the telephone was shaking, the wooden jetty was shaking, the wind had turned cold, the wind that was blowing between the jetty's pilings and ruffling the surface of those interminable, darkening waves, and then Jack said, It's been such a long time, Joanna, great to hear your voice, and I said, It's great to hear yours, Jack, and then I stopped shaking and stopped looking down and looked at the horizon, the lights of the restaurants along the beach—red, blue, yellow—which seemed sad at first but comforting too, and then Jack said, When can I see you, Joannie, and I didn't realize straightaway that he had called me Joannie, for a couple of seconds I was floating on air like I was high or weaving a chrysalis around myself, but then I realized and laughed and Jack knew why I was laughing without needing to ask or needing me to tell him anything. Whenever you like, Jack, I replied. Well, he said, I don't know if you've heard that I'm not as well as I used to be. Are you on your own, Jack? Yes, he said, I'm always on my own. Then I hung up and asked Robbie and Ronnie how to get to Jack's place, and they said I was bound to get lost, and shouldn't even think of spending the night because we were shooting early the next day, and I probably wouldn't be able to get a taxi to take me there, Jack lived near Monrovia, in a shabby old bungalow that was practically falling down, and I told them I wanted to go see Jack however hard it might be, and Robbie said, Take my Porsche, you can have it as long as you turn up on time tomorrow, and I kissed Ronnie and Robbie and got into the Porsche and started driving through the streets of Los Angeles, which had just begun to succumb to the night, the cloak of night falling, like in a song by Nicola Di Bari, or the wheels of the night rolling on, and I didn't want to put on any music, though I have to admit I was tempted by Robbie's sound system—CD or laser-disc or ultrasound or something—but I didn't need music, it was enough to step on the accelerator and feel the hum of the engine; I must have got lost at least a dozen times, and the hours went by and every time I asked someone the best way to get to Monrovia I felt freer, like I didn't care if I spent the whole night driving around in the Porsche, and twice I even caught myself singing, and finally I got to Pasadena, and from there I took Highway 210 to Monrovia, where I spent another hour looking for Jack's place, and when I found his bungalow, after midnight, I sat in the car for a while, unable and unwilling to get out, looking at myself in the mirror, with my hair in a mess and my face as well, my eyeliner had run and my lipstick was smudged and there was dust from the road on my cheeks, as if I'd run all the way and not come in Robbie Pantoliano's Porsche, or as if I'd been crying, but in fact my eyes were dry (a little bit red, maybe, but dry), and my hands were steady and I felt like laughing, as if my food at the beachside restaurant had been spiked with some kind of drug, and I'd only just realized and accepted that I was high or extremely happy. And then I got out of the car, put on the alarm—it didn't feel like a very safe neighborhood—and headed for the bungalow, which matched Robbie's description: a little house crying out for a coat of paint, with a rickety porch; a pile of boards that was practically falling down, but next to it there was a swimming pool, and although it was very small, the water was clean, I could see that straightaway because the pool light was on; I remember thinking that Jack had given up waiting for me or had fallen asleep, because there were no lights on in the house; the boards on the porch creaked under my feet; there was no bell, so I knocked twice on the door, first with my knuckles and then with the palm of my hand, and a light came on, I could hear someone saying something inside, and then the door opened and Jack appeared on the threshold, taller than ever, thinner than ever, and said, Joannie? as if he didn't recognize me or still hadn't completely woken up, and I said, Yes, Jack, it's me, it was hard to find you but I found you in the end, and we hugged. That night we talked until three in the morning and Jack fell asleep at least twice during the conversation. Although he looked drained and weak, he was making an effort to keep his eyes open. But in the end he was just too tired and he said he was going to bed. I don't have a spare room, Joannie, he said, so you choose: my bed or the sofa. Your bed, I said, with you. Good, he said, let's go. He took a bottle of tequila and we went to his bedroom. I hadn't seen such a messy room for years. Do you have an alarm clock? I asked him. No, Joannie, there are no clocks in this house, he said. Then he switched off the light, took off his clothes and got into bed. I stood there watching him, not moving. Then I went to the window and opened the curtains, hoping that the light of dawn would wake me up. When I got into bed, Jack seemed to be asleep, but he wasn't, he drank another shot of tequila and then he said something I couldn't understand. I put my hand on his stomach and stroked it until he fell asleep. Then I moved my hand down a bit and touched his cock, which was big and cold like a python. A few hours later I woke up, took a shower, made breakfast, and I even had time to tidy up the living room and the kitchen a bit. We had breakfast in bed. Jack seemed happy that I was there, but all he had was coffee. I said I'd come back that evening, I told him to expect me, I wouldn't be late this time, and he said, I've got nothing to do Joannie, you can come whenever you like. It was almost like saying, It's OK if you never come back, I knew that, but I decided that Jack needed me and that I needed him too. Who are you working with? he asked. Shane Bogart, I said. He's a good kid, said Jack. We worked together once, I think it was when he was just starting out in the business; he's enthusiastic, and he doesn't like to make trouble. Yeah, he's a good kid, I said. And where are you working? In Venice? Yeah, I said, in the same old house. But you know old Adolfo got killed? Of course I know, Jack, that was years ago. I haven't been working much lately, he said. Then I gave him a kiss, a schoolgirl's kiss on his narrow, chapped lips, and I left. The trip back was much quicker; the sun was running with me, the California morning sun, which has a metallic edge to it. And from then on, after each day of shooting, I'd go to Jack's house or we'd go out together; Jack had an old station wagon and I rented a two-seater Alfa Romeo, and we'd drive off into the mountains, to Redlands, and then on Highway 10 to Palm Springs, Palm Desert, Indio, until we got to the Salton Sea, which is a lake, not a sea (and not a very pretty one either), where we ate macrobiotic food, that's what Jack was eating then, for his health, he said, and one day we stepped on the gas in my Alfa and drove to Calipatria, to the southeast of the Salton Sea, and went to see a friend of Jack's who lived in a bungalow that was even more run-down than the one Jack lived in, Graham Monroe was the guy's name, but his wife and Jack called him Mezcalito, I don't know why, maybe because he was partial to mescal, though all they drank while we were there was beer (I didn't have any—beer is fattening), and the three of them went and sunbathed behind the bungalow and hosed each other down, and I put on my bikini and watched them, I prefer not to get too much sun, my skin's very fair and I like to take care of it, but even though I stayed in the shade and didn't let them wet me with the hose, I was glad to be there, watching Jack, his legs were much thinner than I remembered, and his chest seemed to have sunken in, only his cock was the same, and his eyes too, but no, the only thing that hadn't changed was the great jackhammer, as the ads for his movies used to say, the ram that battered Marilyn Chambers' ass; the rest of him, including his eyes, was fading as fast as my Alfa Romeo flying down the Aguanga Valley or across the Desert State Park lit by the glow of a moribund Sunday. I think we made love a couple of times. Jack had lost interest. He said after so many movies he was worn out. No one's ever told me that before, I said. I like watching TV, Joannie, and reading mysteries. You mean horror stories? No, just mysteries, he said, with detectives, especially the ones where the hero dies at the end. But that never happens, I said. Of course it does, little sister, in old pulp novels you can buy by the pound. Actually, I didn't see any books in his house, except for a medical reference book and three of those pulp novels he'd mentioned, which he must have read over and over again. One night, maybe the second night I spent at his house, or the third—Jack was as slow as a snail when it came to opening up and telling secrets—while we were drinking wine by the pool, he said he probably didn't have long to live: You know how it is, Joannie, when your time's up, your time's up. I wanted to shout, Make love to me, let's get married, let's have a kid or adopt an orphan or buy a pet and a trailer and go traveling through California and Mexico—I guess I was tired and a bit drunk, it must have been a hard day on the set—but I didn't say anything, I just shifted uneasily in my deck chair, looked at the lawn that I'd mowed myself, drank some more wine, and waited for Jack to go on and say the words that had to come next, but that was all he said. We made love that night for the first time in so long. It was very hard to get Jack going, his body wasn't working anymore, only his will was still working, but he insisted on wearing a condom, a condom for that cock of his, as if any condom could hold it, at least it gave us a bit of a laugh, and in the end, we both lay on our sides, and he put his long, thick, flaccid cock between my legs, kissed me sweetly and fell asleep, but I stayed awake for ages, with the strangest ideas passing through my mind; there were moments when I felt sad and cried without making a sound so as not to wake him up or break our embrace, and there were moments when I felt happy, and I cried then too and hiccupped, not even trying to restrain myself, squeezing Jack's cock between my thighs and listening to his breathing, saying: Jack, I know you're pretending to be asleep, Jack, open your eyes and kiss me, but Jack went on sleeping or pretending to sleep, and I went on watching the thoughts race through my mind as if across a movie screen, flashing past, like a plow or a red tractor going a hundred miles an hour, leaving me

almost no time to think, not that thinking was high on my
list of priorities, and then there were moments when I wasn't
crying or feeling sad or happy, I just felt alive and I knew that
Jack was alive and although there was a kind of theatrical
backdrop to everything, as if it were all some pleasant, innocent, even decorous farce, I knew it was real and worthwhile,
and then I put my head in the crook of his neck and fell
asleep. One day around midday Jack turned up while we were
shooting. I was on all fours, sucking Bull Edwards while
Shane Bogart sodomized me. At first I didn't realize that Jack
had come onto the set, I was concentrating; it's not easy to
groan with an eight-inch dick moving back and forth in your
mouth; I know really photogenic girls who lose it as soon as
they start a blow job, they look terrible, maybe because they're
too into it, but I like to keep my face looking good. So my
mind was on the job and, anyway, because of the position I
was in, I couldn't see what was happening around me, while
Bull and Shane, who were on their knees, but upright, heads
raised, they saw that Jack had just come in, and their cocks
got harder almost straightaway, and it wasn't just Bull and
Shane who reacted, the director, Randy Cash, and Danny Lo
Bello and his wife and Robbie and Ronnie and the technicians and everyone, I think, except for the cameraman, Jacinto Ventura, who was a bright, cheerful kid and a true
professional, he literally couldn't take his eyes off the scene he
was filming, everyone except for him reacted in some way to
Jack's unexpected presence, and a silence fell over the set, not
a heavy silence, not the kind that foreshadows bad news, but
a luminous silence, so to speak, the silence of water falling in
slow motion, and I sensed the silence and thought it must
have been because I was feeling so good, because of those

beautiful California days, but I also sensed something else, something indecipherable approaching, announced by the rhythmic bumping of Shane's hips on my butt, by Bull's gentle thrusting in my mouth, and then I knew that something was happening on the set, though I didn't look up, and I knew that what was happening involved and revolved around me; it was as if reality had been torn, ripped open from one end to the other, like in those operations that leave a scar from neck to groin, a broad, rough, hard scar, but I hung on and kept concentrating till Shane took his cock out of my ass and came on my butt and just after that Bull ejaculated on my face. Then they turned me over and I could see the expressions on their faces, they were very focused on what they were doing, much more than usual, and as they caressed me and said tender words, I thought, There's something going on here, there must be someone from the industry on the set, some big fish from Hollywood, and Shane and Bull have realized, they're acting for him, and I remember glancing sideways at the silhouettes surrounding us in the shadows, all still, all turned to stone—that was exactly what I thought, they've turned to stone, it must be a really important producer—but I kept quiet, I wasn't ambitious the way Shane and Bull were, I think it has something to do with being European, we have a different outlook, but I also thought, Maybe it isn't a producer, maybe an angel has come onto the set, and that was when I saw him. Jack was next to Ronnie, smiling at me. And then I saw the others: Robbie, the technicians, Danny Lo Bello and his wife, Jennifer Pullman, Margo Killer, Samantha Edge, two guys in dark suits, Jacinto Ventura, who wasn't looking into the viewfinder, and it was only then that I realized he wasn't filming anymore, and for a second or a minute we all froze, as if we'd lost the capacity to speak and move, and the only one smiling (though he was quiet too) was Jack, whose presence seemed to sanctify the set, or that's what I thought later, much later on, remembering that scene again and again: he seemed to be sanctifying our movie and our work and our lives. Then the minute came to an end, another minute began, someone said it was a wrap, someone brought bathrobes for Bull and Shane and me, Jack came over and gave me a kiss; I wasn't in the other scenes they were shooting that day, so I said let's go and have dinner in an Italian restaurant, I'd heard about one on Figueroa Street, and Robbie invited us to a party that one of his new business partners was throwing; Jack seemed reluctant but I convinced him in the end. So we went back to my place in the Alfa Romeo and talked and drank whiskey for a while, and then we went out to dinner and at about eleven we turned up at the party. Everyone was there and they all knew Jack or came over to be introduced to him. And then Jack and I went to his place and watched TV in the living room—there was a silent movie on—and kissed until we fell asleep. He didn't come back to the set. I had another week's work there, but I'd already decided to stay in Los Angeles for a while after the end of the shoot. Of course I had commitments in Italy and France, but I thought I could put them off, or I thought I'd be able to convince Jack to come with me; he'd been to Italy a number of times, he'd made some movies with La Cicciolina, which had been big hits—some with just me, and some with both of us; Jack liked Italy, so one night I told him what I was thinking. But I had to give up on that idea or hope, I had to wrench it out of my head and heart, or out of my cunt, as the women say back in Torre del Greco, and although I never completely gave up, somehow I understood Jack's reluctance or his stubbornness, the luminous, fresh, honey-slow silence surrounding him and his few words, as if his tall thin figure were vanishing, and all of California along with it; in spite of my happiness, my joy, or what until shortly before I had thought of as happiness and joy, he was going, and I understood that his departure or farewell was a kind of solidification: strange, oblique, almost secret, but still a solidification, and the understanding, the certainty (if that's what it was) made me happy and yet at the same time it made me cry, it made me keep fixing my eye make-up and made me see everything differently, as if I had X-ray vision, and that power or superpower made me nervous, but I liked it too; it was like being Marvilla, the daughter of the Queen of the Amazons, although Marvilla had dark hair and mine is blonde, and one afternoon, in Jack's yard, I saw something on the horizon, I don't know what, clouds, a bird of some kind, a plane, and I felt a pain so strong I fainted and lost control of my bladder and when I woke up I was in Jack's arms and I looked into his grey eyes and began to cry and didn't stop crying for a long time. Robbie and Ronnie came to the airport to see me off along with Danny Lo Bello and his wife, who were planning to visit Italy in a few months' time. I said good-bye to Jack at his bungalow in Monrovia. Don't get up, I said, but he got up and came to the door with me. Be a good girl, Joannie, he said, and write me some time. I'll call you, I said, it's not the end of the world. He was nervous and forgot to put on his shirt. I didn't say anything; I picked up my bag and put it on the passenger seat of the Alfa Romeo. I don't know why I thought that when I turned back to look at him for the last time he'd be gone and the space he'd occupied next to the rickety little wooden gate would be empty, so fear made me delay that moment, it was the first time I'd felt afraid in Los Angeles (on that visit I mean; there'd been plenty of fear and boredom the other times) and I was annoyed to be feeling afraid, and I didn't want to turn around until I had opened the door of the Alfa Romeo and was ready to get in and drive away fast, and when I did finally open the door, I turned and Jack was there, standing by the gate, watching me, and then I knew that everything was all right, and I could go. That everything was all wrong, and I could go. That everything was sorrow, and I could go. And while the detective watches me out of the corner of his eye (he's pretending to look at the foot of the bed, but I know he's looking at my legs, my long legs underneath the sheets) and talks about a cameraman who worked with Mancuso or Marcantonio, a certain R. P. English, poor Marcantonio's second cameraman, I know that in some sense I'm still in California, on my last trip to California, although I didn't know that at the time, and Jack is still alive and looking at the sky, sitting on the edge of the pool with his feet dangling in the water, in the void, the misty synthesis of our love and our separation. And what did this man called English do? I ask the detective. He would prefer not to answer, but faced with my steady gaze, he replies: Terrible things, and then he looks at the floor, as if it were forbidden to say those words in the Clinique Les Trapèzes, in Nîmes, as if I hadn't been acquainted with some terrible things in my time. And at this point I could press him for more, but why spoil such a beautiful afternoon by obliging him to tell what would surely be a sad story. And anyway the photo he has shown me of the man presumed to be English is old and blurry, it shows a young man of twenty-something, and the

English I remember was well into his thirties, maybe even over forty, a definite shadow, if you'll pardon the paradox, a broken shadow; I didn't pay much attention to him, although his features have remained in my memory: blue eyes, prominent cheekbones, full lips, small ears. But describing him like that gives a false impression. I met R. P. English on one of my many shoots around Italy, but his face receded into the shadows long ago. And the detective says, It's all right, don't worry, take your time, Madame Silvestri, at least you remember him, even that is useful, now I know for sure he's not a ghost. And I'm tempted to tell him that we are all ghosts, that all of us have gone too soon into the world of ghost movies, but he's a good man and I don't want to hurt him, so I keep it to myself. Anyway, who's to say he doesn't already know?

PREFIGURATION OF LALO CURA

I t's hard to believe, but I was born in a neighborhood called Los Empalados: The Impaled. The name glows like the moon. The name opens a way through the dream with its horn and man follows that path. A quaking path. Invariably harsh. The path that leads into or out of hell. That's what it all comes down to. Getting closer to hell or further away. Me, for example, I've had people killed. I've given the best birthday presents. I've backed projects of epic proportions. I've opened my eyes in the dark. Once I opened them by slow degrees in total darkness and all I saw or imagined was that name: Los Empalados, shining like the star of destiny. I'll tell you everything, naturally. My father was a renegade priest. I don't know if he was Colombian or came from some other country. But he was Latin American. He turned up one night stone broke in Medellín, preaching sermons in bars and whorehouses. Some people thought he was working for the secret police, but my mother kept him from getting killed and took him to her penthouse in the neighborhood. They lived together for four months, I've been told, and then my father vanished into the Gospels. Latin America was calling him, and he kept slipping away into the sacrificial words until he vanished, gone without a trace. Whether he was a Catholic priest or a Protestant minister is something I'll never find out now. I know that he was alone and that he moved among the masses, fevered and loveless, full of passion and empty of hope. I was named Olegario when I was born, but people have always called me Lalo. My father was known as El Cura, the priest, and that's what my mother wrote down next to *surname* at the registry office. It's my official name. Olegario Cura. I was even baptized into the Catholic faith. She sure was a dreamer, my mother. Connie Sánchez was her name, and if you weren't so young and innocent, it would ring a bell. She was one of the stars of the Olimpo Movie Production Company. The other two stars were Doris Sánchez, my mother's younger sister, and Monica Farr, née Leticia Medina, from Valparaíso. Three good friends. The Olimpo Movie Production Company specialized in pornography, and although the business was more or less illegal and operating in a distinctly hostile environment, it didn't go under until the mid-eighties. The guy in charge was a multi-talented German, Helmut Bittrich, who worked as the company's manager, director, set designer, composer, publicist and, occasionally, thug. Sometimes he even acted, under the name of Abelardo Bello. He was a weird guy, Bittrich. No one had ever seen him with an erection. He liked to do weights at the Health and Friendship Gym, but he wasn't gay. It's just that in the movies he never fucked anyone. Male or female. If you can be bothered, you'll find him playing a Peeping Tom, a schoolteacher, a spy in a seminary—always a modest, minor role. What he liked best was playing a doctor. A German doctor, of course, although most of the time he didn't even open his mouth: he was Doctor Silence. The blue-eyed doctor hidden behind a conveniently located velvet curtain. Bittrich had a house on the outskirts of town, where the neighborhood of Los Empalados borders the wasteland, El Gran Baldío. The cottage in the movies. The house of solitude, which was later to become the house of crime, out there on its own, among clumps of trees and blackberry bushes. Connie used to take me. I'd stay in the yard playing with the dogs and the geese, which the German reared there as if they were his children. There were flowers growing wild among the weeds and the dogs' dirt holes. In the course of a regular morning ten to fifteen people would go into that house. Although the windows were shut you could hear the moans coming from inside. Sometimes there was laughter too. At lunchtime Connie and Doris would take a folding table out into the backyard, under a tree, and the employees of the Olimpo Movie Production Company would hoe into the canned food that Bittrich heated up on a gas ring. They ate directly from the cans or off cardboard plates. Once I went into the kitchen, to help, and when I opened the cupboards all I found were enema tubes, hundreds of enema tubes lined up as if for a military parade. Everything in the kitchen was fake. There were no real plates, no real knives and forks, no real pots and pans. That's what it's like in the movies, said Bittrich, watching me with those blue eyes of his—they scared me then, but thinking of them now I just feel sad. The kitchen was fake. Everything in the house was fake. Who sleeps here at night? Sometimes Uncle Helmut does, Connie replied. Uncle Helmut stays here to look after the dogs and the geese and get on with his work. Editing his homemade movies. Homemade, but the business was booming: the films went out to Germany, Holland and Switzerland. Some copies stayed in

Latin America and others were sold in the United States, but most of them went to Europe, which is where Bittrich had his main client base. Maybe that's why he did a voice-over in German, narrating the various scenes. Like a travel journal for sleepwalkers. And the obsession with mother's milk, another European peculiarity. When Connie was pregnant with me, she went on working. And Bittrich made lacto-porn. Along the lines of Milch and Pregnant Fantasies, aimed at men who believe or make believe that women lactate during pregnancy. With her eight-month bulge, Connie squeezed her breasts and the milk flowed like lava. She leaned over Pajarito Gómez or Sansón Fernández or both of them and gave them a good swig of milk. That was one of the German's tricks; Connie never had milk. Or only a little bit, for two weeks, maybe three, just enough to give me a taste. But that was all. Actually the movies were like Pregnant Fantasies, not so much like Milch. There's Connie, big and blonde, with me curled up inside her, laughing as she lubricates Pajarito Gómez's asshole with Vaseline. She already has the sure, delicate movements of a mother. My moron of a father has left her and there she is, with Doris and Monica Farr, and the three of them are smiling on and off, exchanging looks and subtle signals or secrets among themselves, while Pajarito stares at her belly as if in a hypnotic trance. The mystery of life in Latin America. Like a little bird charmed by the gaze of a snake. The Force is with me, I thought, the first time I saw that movie, at the age of nineteen, crying my eyes out, grinding my teeth, pinching the sides of my head, the Force is with me. All dreams are real. I wanted to believe that when those cocks had gone as far into my mother as they could, they came up against my eyes. I often dreamed about that: my sealed, translucent eyes swimming in the black soup of life. Life? No: the dealing that imitates life. My squinting eyes, like the snake hypnotizing the little bird. You get the picture: a kid's silly celluloid fantasies. All fake, as Bittrich used to say. And he was right, as he almost always was. That's why the girls adored him. They were glad to have the German around; they could always count on him for friendly advice and comfort. The girls: Connie, Doris and Monica. Three good friends lost in the mists of time. Connie tried to make it on Broadway. Even in the hardest years, I don't think she ever gave up on the possibility of happiness. There, in New York, she met Monica Farr and they shared their hardships and hopes. They cleaned hotel rooms, sold their blood, turned tricks. Always looking for a break, walking around the city hooked up to the same Walkman, typical dancers, a little bit thinner and closer together with every passing day. Chorus girls. Looking for Bob Fosse. At a party thrown by some Colombians they met Bittrich, who was passing through New York with a batch of his merchandise. They talked until dawn. No sex, just music and words. They cast their dice that night on Seventh Avenue, the Prussian artist and the Latin American whores. It was all decided then and there. In some of my nightmares I see myself resting in limbo again and then I hear, distantly at first, the sound of the dice on the pavement. I open my eyes and I scream. Something changed forever that morning. The bond of friendship took hold, like the plague. Then Connie and Monica Farr got an acting job in Panama, where they were thoroughly exploited. The German paid for their tickets to Medellín, which was home to Connie and as good a place as any for Monica. There are photos of them descending the steps from the plane, taken by Doris, the only person who went to meet them at the airport. Connie and Monica are wearing sunglasses and tight pants. They're not very tall, but they're well proportioned. The Medellín sun is casting long shadows across an airstrip devoid of planes, except for one in the background, emerging from a hangar. There are no clouds in the sky. Connie and Monica displaying their teeth. Drinking Coca-Cola in the taxi line and striking provocative, turbulent poses. Atmospheric and terrestrial turbulence. Their attitude suggests that they have come straight from New York, surrounded by mystery. Then a very young Doris appears beside them. The three of them hugging each other, photographed by an obliging stranger leaning against the taxi's bumper, while the driver inside looks on, so old and worn it's hard to believe he's real. So begin the most passionate adventures. A month later they are already shooting the first movie: *Hecatomb*. While the world is in turmoil the German shoots *Hecatomb*. A film about the turmoil of the spirit. A saint in prison remembers nights of plenitude and fucking. Connie and Monica do it with four guys who look like shadows. Doris walks along the bank of a weakly flowing river accompanied by Bittrich's largest goose. The night is unusually starry. At dawn, Doris comes across Pajarito Gómez and they start making love in the back part of Bittrich's house. There is a great fluttering of geese. Connie and Monica at a window, clapping. The lobster-red cock of the saint shines with semen. The End. The credits appear over the image of a sleeping policeman. Bittrich's sense of humor. His movies amused drug lords and businessmen. The ordinary guys, the gunmen and the messengers, didn't understand them; they'd have been quite happy to blow the German away. Another movie: *Kundalini*. A rancher's wake. While the mourners weep and drink coffee with aguardiente, Connie enters a dark room full of farming implements. Two guys—one disguised as a bull and one as a condor—jump out of an enormous wardrobe. They proceed to force Connie's front and rear entries. Connie's lips curve into the shape of a letter. Monica and Doris touching each other up in the kitchen. Then stables full of cattle and a man approaching with difficulty, pushing his way through the cows. It's Pajarito Gómez. He never arrives: the following scene shows him stretched out in the mud, among cowpats and hooves. Monica and Doris rimming each other on a big white bed. The dead rancher opens his eyes. He sits up and climbs out of the coffin to the horror and amazement of his family and friends. Covered by the bull and the condor, Connie pronounces the word *Kundalini*. The cows escape from the stables and the credits appear over the abandoned, gradually darkening body of Pajarito Gómez. Another movie: *Impluvium*. Two genuine beggars dragging sacks along a dirt road. They reach the backyard of Bittrich's house. There they find Monica Farr, completely naked and chained in an upright position. The beggars empty the sacks: an abundant collection of sexual instruments made of steel and leather. The beggars put on masks with phallic protuberances, and, kneeling down, one in front of Monica, one behind, they penetrate her, moving their heads in a way that is, to say the least, ambiguous: it's hard to tell whether they're excited or the masks are suffocating them. Lying on an army camp bed, Pajarito Gómez smokes a cigarette. On another camp bed the conscript Sansón Fernandez is jerking off. The camera pans slowly over Monica's face: she is crying. The beggars depart, dragging their sacks down a miserable, unpaved street. Still chained, Monica shuts her eyes and seems to fall asleep. She dreams of the masks, the latex noses, the pair of old carcasses who could barely hold a breath of air and yet were so enthusiastic in the performance of their task. Supernatural carcasses emptied of all the essentials. Then Monica gets dressed, walks through the centre of Medellín, and is invited to an orgy, where she meets Connie and Doris; they kiss and smile at each other, and talk about what they've been doing. Pajarito Gómez, half dressed in fatigues, has fallen asleep. When the orgy is over, before it gets dark, the owner of the house wants to show them his most prized possession. The girls follow their host to a garden covered with a metal and glass canopy. The man's bejeweled finger indicates something at the far end. The girls examine a cement swimming pool in the shape of a coffin. When they lean over the edge, they see their faces reflected in the water. Then dusk falls and the beggars come to an area where big cargo ships are docked. The music, performed by a band of kettledrummers, gets louder, more sinister and ominous, until the storm finally breaks. Bittrich adored sound effects like that. Thunder in the mountains, the sizzle of lightning, splintering trees, rain against window panes. He collected them on high quality tapes. He said it was to make his movies atmospheric, but in fact it was just because he liked the effects. The full range of sounds that rain makes in a forest. The rhythmic or random sibilance of the wind and the sea. Sounds to make you feel alone, sounds to make your hair stand on end. His great treasure was the roar of a hurricane. I heard it as a kid. The actors were drinking coffee under a tree and Bittrich was playing with an enormous German tape player, away from the others, looking pasty, the way he did when he'd been working too hard. Now you're going to hear the hurricane from inside, he said. At first I couldn't hear anything. I think I was expecting a god-almighty, ear-splitting racket, so I was disappointed when all I could hear was a kind of intermittent whirling. An intermittent ripping. Like a propeller made of meat. Then I heard voices; it wasn't the hurricane, of course, but the pilots of the plane flying in its eye. Hard voices talking in Spanish and English. Bittrich was smiling as he listened. Then I heard the hurricane again and this time I really heard it. Emptiness. A vertical bridge and emptiness, emptiness, emptiness. I'll never forget the smile on Bittrich's face. It was as if he was weeping. Is that all? I asked, not wanting to admit that I'd already had enough. That's all, said Bittrich, fascinated by the silently turning reels. Then he stopped the tape player, closed it up very carefully, went inside with the others and got back to work. Another movie: *Ferryman*. From the ruins you might think it's about life in Latin America after the Third World War. The girls wander through garbage dumps, along deserted paths. Then there's a broad, gently flowing river. Pajarito Gómez and two other guys play cards by the light of a candle. The girls come to an inn where the men are carrying guns. They make love with them all, one after another. They look out from the bushes at the river and a few pieces of wood tied clumsily together. Pajarito Gómez is the ferryman, at least that's what everyone calls him, but he doesn't budge from the table. He holds the best cards. The villains remark on how well he's playing. What a good player the ferryman is. What good luck the ferryman has. Gradually the supplies begin to run short. The cook and the kitchen hand torture Doris, penetrating her with the handles of enormous butcher's knives. Hunger reigns over the inn: some stay in bed, others wander through the bushes looking for food. While the men fall ill one by one, the girls scribble in their diaries as if possessed. Desperate pictograms. Images of the river superimposed on images of a never-ending orgy. The end is predictable. The men dress the women up as chickens, make them do their tricks, and then proceed to eat them at a feather-strewn banquet. The bones of Connie, Monica and Doris lie on the diner's patio. Pajarito Gómez plays another hand of poker. He wears his luck like a close-fitting glove. The camera is behind him and the viewer can see the cards he's holding. They are blank. The credits appear over the corpses of all the actors. Three seconds before the end of the film, the river changes color, turning jet black. That one was especially deep, Doris used to say, it illustrates the sad fate of artists in the porn industry: first we're ruthlessly exploited, then we're devoured by thoughtless strangers. Bittrich seems to have made that movie to compete with the cannibal porn videos that were starting to cause a stir at the time. But it isn't hard to see that the film's real center is Pajarito Gómez sitting in the gambling den. Pajarito Gómez, who could generate an inner vibration that planted his image in the viewer's eyes. A great actor wasted by life, our life, yours and mine, my friends. But the movies Bittrich made live on, unsullied. And so does Pajarito Gómez, holding those cards covered with dust, with his dirty hands and his dirty neck, his eternally half-closed eyelids, vibrating on and on. Pajarito Gómez, an emblematic figure in the pornography of the 1980s. He wasn't specially well endowed or muscular, he didn't appeal to the target audience for that kind of movie. He looked like Walter Abel. He had no experience when Bittrich dragged him from the gutter and put him in front of a camera: the rest came so naturally it's hard to believe. Pajarito had this continuous vibration, and watching him, sooner or later, depending on your powers of resistance, you'd be suddenly transfixed by the energy emanating from that scrap of a man, who looked so feeble. So unprepossessing, so undernourished. So strangely triumphant. The preeminent porn actor in Bittrich's Colombian cycle. The best when it came to playing dead and the best when it came to playing vacant. He was also the only member of the German's cast who survived: in 1999, the only one still alive was Pajarito Gómez, the rest had been killed or succumbed to disease. Sansón Fernández died of AIDS. Praxíteles Barrionuevo died in the Hole of Bogotá. Ernesto San Román was stabbed to death in the Areanea sauna in Medellín. Alvarito Fuentes died of AIDS in the Cartago jail. All of them young guys with supersize cocks. Frank Moreno, shot to death in Panama. Oscar Guillermo Montes, shot to death in Puerto Berrío. David Salazar, known as the Anteater, shot to death in Palmira. Victims of vendettas or fortuitous brawls. Evelio Latapia, hung in a hotel room in Popayán. Carlos José Santelices, stabbed by strangers in an alley in Maracaibo. Reinaldo Hermosilla, last seen in El Progreso, Honduras. Dionisio Aurelio Pérez, shot to death in a bar in Mexico City. Maximiliano Moret, drowned in the Marañon River. Ten- to twelve-inch cocks, sometimes so long they couldn't get them up. Young mestizos, blacks, whites, Indians, sons of Latin America, whose only assets were a pair of balls and a member tanned by exposure to the elements or miraculously pink by some weird freak of nature. The sadness of the phallus was something Bittrich understood better than anyone. I mean the sadness of those monumental members against the backdrop of this vast and desolate continent. For example, Oscar Guillermo Montes in a scene from a movie I've forgotten the rest of; he's naked from the waist down, his penis hangs flaccid and dripping. It's dark and wrinkled and the drops have a milky sheen. Behind the actor a landscape unfolds: mountains, ravines, rivers, forests, ranges, towering clouds, a city perhaps, a volcano, a desert. Oscar Guillermo Montes perched on a high ridge, an icy breeze playing with a lock of his hair. That's all. It's like a poem by Tablada, isn't it? But you've never heard of Tablada. Neither had Bittrich, and it doesn't matter, really, it's all there in that image—I must have the tape around somewhere—the loneliness I was talking about. Impossible geography, impossible anatomy. What was Bittrich aiming for with that sequence? Was he trying to justify amnesia, our amnesia? Or portray Oscar Guillermo's weary eyes? Or did he just want to show us an uncircumcised penis dripping in the continent's immensity? Or give an impression of useless grandeur: handsome young men without shame, marked out for sacrifice, fated to disappear in the immensity of chaos? Who knows? The only one who always got away was the amateur Pajarito Gómez, whose endowment extended, after plenty of work, to a maximum length of seven inches. The German flirted with death—what the hell did he care about death?—he flirted with solitude and black holes, but he never tried anything with Pajarito. Elusive and uncontrollable, Pajarito came into the camera's scope as if he just happened to be passing by and had stopped for a look. Then he began to vibrate, full on, and the viewers, whether they were solitary jerk-off artists or businessmen who used the videos to liven up the decor, barely intending to glance at them, were transfixed by that scrawny creature's moods. Pajarito Gómez gave off prostatic fluid! And that was something different, far exceeding the German's lucubrations. And Bittrich knew it, so when Pajarito appeared in a scene there were usually no additional effects, no music or sounds of any kind, nothing to distract the viewer from what really mattered: the hieratic Pajarito Gómez, sucked or sucking, fucking or fucked, but always vibrating, as if unawares. The German's protectors were deeply suspicious of that talent; they'd have preferred to see Pajarito working in the central market unloading trucks, ruthlessly exploited until the day he disappeared. They wouldn't have been able to explain what it was they didn't like about him; they just had a vague sense that he was a guy who could attract bad luck and make people feel ill at ease. Sometimes, when I remember my childhood, I wonder how Bittrich must have felt about his protectors. He respected the drug lords; after all they put up the money, and like all good Europeans, he respected money, a point of reference in the midst of chaos. But the corrupt police and army officers, what would he have thought of them, Bittrich, a German, who read history books in his spare time? They must have seemed so ludicrous, he must have had such a good laugh at them, at night, after those unruly meetings. Monkeys in SS uniforms, that's what they were. Alone in his house, surrounded by his videos and his amazing sounds, he must have laughed and laughed. And they were the ones who wanted to get rid of Pajarito, those monkeys, with their sixth sense. Those pathetic, odious monkeys thought they could tell him, a German director in permanent exile, who he should and shouldn't be hiring. Imagine Bittrich after one of those meetings, in the dark house in Los Empalados, after everyone else has gone, drinking rum and smoking Mexican Delicados in the biggest room, the one he uses as his study and bedroom. On the table there are paper cups with dregs of whiskey in them. Two or three videotapes sitting on top of the TV, the latest from the Olimpo Movie Production Company. Diaries and torn-out pages covered with figures: salaries, bribes, bonuses. Pocket money. And the words of the police commissioner, the air force lieutenant and the colonel from military intelligence still floating in the air: We don't want that jinx anywhere near the Company. When people see him in our films, their stomachs turn. It's bad taste to have that slug fucking the girls. And Bittrich let them speak, he observed them silently, and then he did what he liked. After all, they were only porn videos; it's not like there were serious profits at stake. And that was how Pajarito got to stay on with us, although the company's backers found his presence disturbing. Pajarito Gómez. A quiet and pretty reserved sort of guy, but for some mysterious reason the girls were especially fond of him. In the course of their professional duties, they all got to lay him, and it left them with a curious feeling, hard to say just what it was, but they were all ready to do it again. I guess being with Pajarito was like being nowhere. Doris even ended up living with him for a while, but it didn't work out. Doris and Pajarito: for six months they went back and forth between the Hotel Aurora, which is where he lived, and the apartment on Avenida de los Libertadores. It was too good to last, you know how it is: singular spirits can't bear so much love, so much perfection stumbled on by chance. Maybe if Doris hadn't been such a bombshell, and if she'd been mute, and if Pajarito had never vibrated . . . Things finally fell apart during the shooting of *Cocaine*, one of Bittrich's worst movies. But they stayed friends until the end. Many years later, when all the rest were dead, I tracked down Pajarito. He was living in a tiny, one-room apartment, on a street that led down to the sea, in Buenaventura. He was working as a waiter in a restaurant owned by a retired policeman: Octopus Ink, the place was called, ideal for someone who wanted to lie low. He went from home to work and back again, with a brief stop each day at a video store, where he'd usually rent a couple of movies. Walt Disney and old Colombian, Mexican or Venezuelan films. Every day, punctual as a clock. From his walk-up to Octopus Ink, and then, after dark, back to the apartment, with two videotapes under his arm. He never brought food back, only movies. He rented them on the way there or the way back, it varied, but always from the same store, a little shack, three yards by three, open eighteen hours a day. I went looking for him on a whim, just because I felt like it. I went looking and I found him in 1999; it was easy, it took less than a week. Pajarito was forty-nine then, but he looked at least ten years older. He wasn't surprised to find me sitting on his bed when he got home. I told him who I was, reminded him of the movies he'd made with my mother and my aunt. Pajarito took a chair and as he sat down the videos fell out from under his arm. You've come to kill me, Lalito, he said. He'd rented films with Ignacio López Tarso and Matt Dillon, two of his favorite actors. I reminded him of the old Pregnant Fantasies days. We both smiled. I saw your prick, it was transparent like a worm; my eyes were open, you know, watching your glass eye. Pajarito nodded, then sniffed. You always were a clever kid, he said, before you were born too, I guess, with your eyes open already, why not. I saw you, that's what matters, I said. You were pink for a start in there, then you turned transparent and you got one hell of a shock, Pajarito. Back then you weren't afraid, you moved so fast only little creatures and fetuses could see you moving. Only cockroaches, nits, lice and fetuses. Pajarito was looking at the floor. I heard him whisper: Et cetera, et cetera. Then he said: I never liked that sort of movie, one or two is OK, but it's criminal to make so many. I'm a fairly normal person, really. I was genuinely fond of Doris, I was always a friend to your mother, when you were little I never did you any harm. Do you remember? I didn't run the business, I never betrayed anyone, or killed anyone. I did a bit of dealing, a few robberies, we all did, but as you can see, it didn't set me up for retirement. Then he picked the videos up off the floor, put the one with Ignacio López Tarso in the VCR, and as the soundless images succeeded one another on the screen, he began to cry. Don't cry, Pajarito, I said, it's not worth it. His days of vibrating were over. Or maybe he was still vibrating a little, and as I sat there on the bed I was scavenging those remnants of energy with the ravenous hunger of a shipwrecked sailor. It's hard to vibrate in such a small apartment, with the smell of chicken soup permeating every cranny. It's hard to pick up a vibration when your eyes are fixed on a dumbly gesticulating Ignacio López Tarso. López Tarso's eyes in black and white: how could so much innocence and so much malice be combined? A good actor, I remarked, just to say something. One of our founding fathers, said Pajarito in agreement. He was right. Then he whispered: Et cetera, et cetera. That lousy fucking Pajarito. We sat there in silence for a long time: López Tarso went gliding through the movie's plot like a fish inside a whale; the images of Connie, Doris and Monica lit up for few seconds in my head, and Pajarito's vibration became imperceptible. I haven't come to rub you out, I said to him in the end. Back then, when I was young, I had trouble using the word *kill*. I never killed: I took people out, blew them away, put them to sleep, I topped, stiffed or wasted them, sent them to meet their maker, made them bite the dust, I iced them, snuffed them, did them in. I smoked people. But I didn't smoke Pajarito, I just wanted to see him and chat for a while. To feel his beat and remember my past. Thanks, Lalito, he said, and then he got up and filled a washbasin with water from a demijohn. With exact, artistic, resigned movements, he washed his hands and his face. When I was a kid, that's what they all called me, Connie, Monica, Doris, Bittrich, Pajarito, Sansón Fernández: they all called me Lalito. Lalito Cura playing in the garden with the dogs and the geese at the house of crime, which for me was the house of boredom and sometimes the house of dismay and happiness. These days there's no time to get bored, happiness vanished somewhere in the world, and all that's left is dismay. Perpetual dismay, composed of corpses and ordinary people, like Pajarito, who was thanking me. I was never intending to kill you, I said, I've kept all your movies, I don't watch them very often, I admit, only on special occasions, but I've looked after them. I'm a collector of your cinematic past, I said. Pajarito sat down again. He had stopped vibrating: he was watching the López Tarso movie out of the corner of his eye and his stillness suggested a mineral patience. According to the clock radio beside the bed it was two in the morning. The night before, I had dreamed of finding Pajarito: I was mounting him and shouting unintelligible words in his ear, something about a buried treasure. Or about an underground city. Or about a dead person wrapped in papers proof against putrefaction and the passage of time. But I didn't even lay my hand on his shoulder. I'll leave you some money, Pajarito, so you can live without having to work. I'll buy you whatever you like. I'll take you to a quiet place where you can spend all your time watching your favorite actors. There was no one like you in Los Empalados, I said. Ignacio López Tarso and Pajarito Gómez looked at me: stone-like patience. The pair of them gone crazily dumb. Their eyes full of humanity and fear and fetuses lost in the immensity of memory. Fetuses and other tiny wide-eyed creatures. For a moment, my friends, I felt that the whole apartment was starting to vibrate. Then I stood up very carefully and left.

MURDERING WHORES

for Teresa Ariño

I saw you on television, Max, and I thought, That's my guy."

(The guy is stubbornly jerking his head, trying to take a deep breath, but he can't.)

"I saw you with your group. Is that what you call it? Maybe you say gang, or crew, but no, I think you say group: it's a simple word and you're a simple man. You'd taken off your tee shirts and you were bare-chested, displaying your young bodies: strong pectorals and biceps, though you'd all like to have more muscle, hairless chests, mostly, but I didn't actually pay much attention to the other chests or bodies, just yours, something about you struck me, your face, your eyes gazing in the direction of the camera (though you probably didn't realize you were being filmed and beamed into our living rooms), the depthless look in your eyes, different from the way they look now, infinitely different from the way they will look soon, eyes that were fixed on glory and happiness, satisfied desire and victory, things that can only exist in the kingdom of the future, things it's better not to hope for because they never come."

(The guy is jerking his head from left to right, still straining for breath and sweating.)

"In fact, seeing you on television was like an invitation. Imagine for a moment that I'm a princess, waiting. An impatient princess. One night I see you, and the reason I see you is that I have, in a sense, been searching, not for you personally but for the prince you are, and what that prince represents. You and your friends are dancing with your tee shirts tied around your necks or your waists. Tied or perhaps furled, a word that according to cranky old nitpickers refers to sails when they're rolled up and bound to a yard or a boom, but in my own young and cranky way, I use it to refer to garments rolled up around the neck or chest or waist. The old and I go our separate ways, as you will have guessed by now. But let's not lose sight of what really interests us. You and your group are young, and all of you are offering your hymns to the night; some of you, the leaders, are brandishing flags. The announcer, poor bastard, is impressed by the tribal dance in which you're taking part. He points it out to the other newsman. They're dancing, he says, in his loutish voice, as if we, the viewers at home, in front of our televisions, hadn't realized. Yes, they're having fun, says the other newsman. Another lout. *They* seem to be enjoying your dance, at least. It's just a conga, really. In the front line there are eight or nine. In the second there are ten. In the third there are seven or eight. In the fourth there are fifteen. United by the team colors and semi-nakedness (tee shirts tied or furled around your waists or necks, or turban-style around your heads) and the dance (if I can call it that) as it moves through the area in which you have been isolated. Your dance is like a lightning bolt in the spring night. The newsman, the newsmen, weary but still able to muster some enthusiasm, salute your initiative. You work your way across the cement steps from the right to the left, and when you reach the wire fence, you go back the other way. The guys at the head of each line are carrying flags, the team flag or the Spanish flag; the rest of you, including the ones at the ends, are waving much smaller flags, or scarves, or the tee shirts you took off earlier. It's a spring night, but it's still cold, and in the end that gives your gesture the force you wanted it to have, the force it merits, after all. Then the lines break up, you start to chant your songs, some of you raise your arms and give the Roman salute. Do you know what it means, that salute? You must, and if you don't, as you raise your arm you can guess. Under my city's night sky you salute in the direction of the television cameras, and watching at home I see you and decide to offer you my salute, in response to yours."

(The guy shakes his head, his eyes seem to fill with tears, his shoulders tremble. Is there love in his gaze? Has his body sensed what will certainly happen, while his mind is still lagging behind? Both phenomena, the tears and the trembling, could result from the effort he is making at this moment, in vain, or from a sincere regret tearing at all his nerves.)

"So, I take off my clothes, I take off my pants, I take off my bra, I take a shower, I put on perfume, I put on clean pants, I put on a clean bra, I put on a black silk top, I put on my best pair of jeans, I put on white socks, I put on my boots, I put on a jacket, the best one I own, and I go into the garden, because to get out into the street, first I have to cross that dark garden, which you especially liked. All in less than ten minutes; normally I'm not so quick. Let's say it's your dance that is speeding up my movements. While I get dressed you're dancing. In some other dimension. Another dimension and another time, like a prince and a princess, like the eruptive call of animals coupling in springtime, I get dressed while, inside the television, you dance wildly with your eyes fixed on something that might be eternity or the key to eternity, except that your eyes as you dance are flat and empty and inexpressive."

(The guy nods repeatedly. What were gestures of denial or desperation are transformed into gestures of affirmation, as if he'd been suddenly seized by an idea, or a *new* idea had just occurred to him.)

"Finally, even though I haven't got time to look at myself in the mirror and check that my clothes are exactly right, and in fact I probably wouldn't want to see my reflection even if I did have time (because what you and I are doing is secret), I go out, leaving just the porch light on, get onto my motorbike and drive through streets where people stranger than you or me are setting out to enjoy their Saturday night, a Saturday to match their expectations, a sad Saturday, in other words, one that will never give life to what they have dreamed and meticulously planned, a Saturday like any other, aggressive and grateful, stocky and affable, perverse and sad. Awful adjectives that aren't my style at all, they make me baulk, but, as always, in the end, I let them stand, as a farewell gesture. My motorbike and I roll on among those lights, those Christian preparations, those baseless expectations, and we come out in front of the stadium, on the Gran Avenida, which is still empty, and we stop beneath the arches of the bridges that lead to the entrance gates, and this is the really strange part: when we stop, I can feel in my legs that the world is still moving, as I suppose you know it does, the earth is moving under my feet, under the wheels of my motorbike, and for a moment, for a fraction of a second, whether or not I find you doesn't matter, you can leave with your friends, you can go and get drunk or take a bus back to the city you come from. But the feeling of abandon, as if I were being fucked by an angel, without penetration—or actually no, penetrated to the core—is brief, and just as I begin to doubt or analyze it in amazement, the gates swing open and the people start coming out of the stadium: a flock of vultures, a flock of crows."

(The guy hangs his head. Lifts it up. His eyes try to smile. His facial muscles are seized by a spasm or a series of spasms that could mean many different things: We're meant for each other, Think of the future, Life is wonderful, Don't do anything stupid, I'm innocent, Spain rules.)

"Finding you is a problem. Will you look the same five yards away as you did on TV? Your height is a problem: I don't know if you're tall or of medium height (you're not short, I know that). Your clothes are a problem: by now it's starting to get cold, and your torso and the torsos of your companions are once again draped in tee shirts or even jackets; some are coming out of the stadium with scarves furled (like sails) around their necks and some are even using their scarves to cover their mouths and cheeks. My footsteps on the cement are lit by vertical moonlight. I search for you patiently, and yet at the same time I am anxious like the princess contemplating the empty frame in which the prince's smile should be shining. Your friends are a problem compounded: they're a temptation. I see them and am seen by them, I am desired, I know they'd pull my jeans off without a second thought; some no doubt deserve my attentions at least as much as you do, but in the end I resist, I remain faithful. Finally you appear, surrounded by conga dancers, chanting the words of a hymn that prefigures our meeting, with a serious look on your face, charged with an importance that no one but you can measure and appreciate precisely; you're tall, quite a lot taller than me, and your arms are long, just as I imagined after seeing you on TV, and when I smile at you, when I say, Hi, Max, you don't know what to say, at first you don't know what to say, you just laugh, not quite as stridently as your friends, but you laugh, my prince of the time machine, you laugh and you stop walking."

(The guy looks at her, narrows his eyes, tries to calm his breathing, and as it becomes more regular, he seems to be thinking: breathe in, breathe out, think, breathe in, breathe out, think . . .)

"Then, instead of saying, I'm not Max, you try to catch up with your group, and for a moment I'm seized by panic, a panic that in retrospect seems closer to laughter than to fear. I follow you without a clear idea of what I am going to do next. But you and three others stop and turn and size me up with cold eyes, and I say, Max, we have to talk, and then you say, I'm not Max, that's not my name, what is this, are you joking, are you getting me mixed up with someone or what, and then I say, Sorry, you really look like Max, and I say, I want to talk with you, What about, Well, about Max, and then you smile, and you finally decide to stay behind and let your friends go off; they shout the name of the bar where you'll meet to set off home, No problem, you say, see you there, and your friends shrink away like the stadium behind us as I drive my bike at full throttle, confidently, and the Gran Avenida is almost empty at this time of night, there are only the people leaving the stadium, and you sit behind me with your arms around my waist, I feel your body against my back like a mollusk clinging to a rock, and it's true that the air on the avenue is cold and dense like the waves that push and pull at the mollusk; you cling to me so naturally, Max, like someone who senses that the sea is not only an inhospitable element but a time tunnel, you furl yourself around my waist the way your tee shirt was furled around your neck, but now the conga is danced by the air that pours like a torrent into the streaky tube that is the Gran Avenida, and you laugh or shout something, maybe you saw some friends among the people sliding past beneath the canopy of trees, maybe you're just yelling insults at strangers, oh Max, you're not shouting Good-bye or Hi or See you, you're shouting slogans that are older than blood, but surely not older than the rock to which you're clinging, happy to feel the waves, the submarine currents of the night, sure that you will not be swept away."

(The guy murmurs something unintelligible. It looks like saliva dripping from his chin, although perhaps it's only sweat. His breathing, in any case, has settled down.)

"And so we arrive at my house on the outskirts of town, safe and sound. You take off your helmet, you touch your balls, you put your arm around my shoulders. The gesture betrays a surprising degree of tenderness and timidity. But your eyes are still not tender and timid enough. You like my house. You like my pictures. You ask me about the figures that appear in them. The Prince and the Princess, I reply. They look like the Catholic Monarchs, you say. Yes, the thought has sometimes occurred to me too, Catholic Monarchs in the confines of their kingdom, Catholic Monarchs spying on each other in a perpetual panic, a perpetual solemnity, but for me, for the person I am at least fifteen hours a day, they are a prince and a princess, a bride and groom who journey through the years, and are wounded, pierced by arrows, who lose their horses on the hunt, or never even had horses and must flee on foot, with only their eyes to guide them, and an idiotic will, which some call kindness and others good nature, as if nature could be qualified, good or bad, wild or tame, nature is nature, Max, that's a fact you have to face, and it will always be there, like an irresolvable mystery, and I'm not talking about forests catching fire but neurons and the left or the right hemisphere of the brain catching fire and blazing for centuries and centuries. But, blessed soul that you are, you think my house is pretty, and you even ask if I'm alone and then you're surprised when I laugh. Do you think I would have invited you here if I hadn't been alone? Do you think I would have ridden right across the city on my motorbike, with you pressed against my back, like a mollusk clinging to a rock, while my head (or my figurehead) plunged through time, with the sole aim of bringing you back safe and sound to this refuge, the real rock, the rock that rears magically from its foundations and breaks the surface, do you think I would have done all that if I hadn't been alone? And just on a practical level, do you think I would have taken an extra helmet, a helmet to protect your face from prying eyes, if my intention hadn't been to bring you back here, into my purest solitude?"

(The guy hangs his head and nods, his eyes scan the walls of the room down to the finest crack. His sweat begins to flow again like a fickle river—or is there a kink in time?—and droplets gather in his eyebrows and hang ominously over his eyes.)

"You don't know anything about painting, Max, but I get the feeling that you know a lot about solitude. You like my Catholic Monarchs, you like beer, you like your country, you like respect, you like your soccer team, you like your friends or buddies or pals, the gang or group or crew, the bunch that saw you stay behind to talk with some hot chick you didn't know, you don't like disorder, you don't like blacks, you don't like faggots, you don't like being treated with disrespect, you don't like getting pushed aside. There are so many things you don't like, in that way you're a lot like me. We're approaching one another, you and I, from opposite ends of the tunnel, and even though all we can see are each other's silhouettes, we keep walking resolutely toward our meeting point. In the middle of the tunnel our arms will be able to intertwine at last, and although the darkness there will be complete, making our faces invisible, I know that we will step forward without fear and touch each other's faces (the first thing you'll touch is my ass, but that too is a part of your desire to know my face), we will feel each other's eyes and perhaps pronounce one or two words of recognition. Then it will be clear (it will become clear to me) that you know nothing about painting, but you do know about solitude, which is almost the same. One day we will meet in the middle of that tunnel, Max, and I will feel your face, your nose, your mouth—which generally expresses your stupidity better than anyone else's—your empty eyes, the tiny folds that form on your cheeks when you smile, the false hardness of your face when you get serious, when you sing your hymns, those hymns you don't understand, your chin that is sometimes rock-like, but more often, I guess, like a vegetable, that chin of yours, Max, which is so typical, so archetypical that now I suspect it's your chin that brought you here, that was your downfall. And then you and I will be able to talk again, or we will talk for the first time, but before that we'll have to roll about, take off our clothes and furl them around our necks, or around the necks of the dead—those who live in the motionless scroll."

(The guy is crying, and it looks like he's trying to speak, but in fact he's just whimpering: the movements of his cheeks and his covered lips are spasms produced by his crying).

"As the gangsters say, it's nothing personal, Max. Of course, that statement contains an element of truth and an element of falsehood. It's always something personal. We have come through a time tunnel unscathed because it's something personal. I chose you because it's something personal. Naturally I had never seen you before. You never did anything to harm me personally. I say that to put your mind at rest. You never raped me. You never raped anyone I know. It's even possible that you never raped anyone at all. It's not something personal. Maybe I'm sick. Maybe all this is a nightmare that neither you nor I is having, although it's hurting you, although the pain is real and personal. And yet I suspect that the end will not be personal. The end: extinction, the gesture that will bring all this irreparably to a close. And personally or impersonally, you and I will enter my house again, and look at my pictures (the Prince and the Princess), drink beer and get undressed, and I will feel your hands again clumsily stroking my back, my ass, my crotch, looking for my clitoris perhaps, but not knowing exactly where it is, I will undress you again, and take your cock in both hands and say, You're so big, when in fact you're not so big, Max, and that is something you ought to know by now, and I'll put it in my mouth again, and suck you like I bet you've never been sucked before, and then I'll take off all your clothes and let you take off mine, one hand busy with my buttons, a glass of whiskey in the other, and I'll look you in the eyes, those eyes I saw on television (and will see again in dreams), the eyes I chose you for, and once again I'll tell you, I'll tell your sickening electric memory that it's nothing personal, and even then I'll have my doubts, I'll feel cold as I do now, I'll try to remember every word you said, even the most insignificant, but none of them will be any consolation."

(The guy jerks his head again, nodding. What is he trying to say? Impossible to tell. His body, or rather his legs, are subject to a curious phenomenon: sometimes they are covered with a sweat as abundant as the sweat on his forehead, especially on the inner sides, sometimes the skin seems to be cold, from the groin to the knees, and takes on a bumpy texture, if not to the touch at least to the eye).

"Your words, I admit, were kind. Nevertheless, I fear that you did not give sufficient thought to what you were saying. And even less to what *I* was saying. You should always listen carefully, Max, to what women say while they're being fucked. If they don't speak, fine, there's nothing to listen to, and you'll probably have nothing to think about, but if they do, even if it's only a murmur, listen to their words and think about them, think about their meanings, think about what they express and leave unexpressed, try to understand what it is they really signify. Women are murdering whores, Max, they're monkeys stiff with cold watching the horizon from a sick tree, they're princesses searching for you in the darkness, crying, examining the words that they will never be able to say. In misunderstanding we live and plan the cycles of our life. For your friends, Max, in that stadium, which is shrinking in your memory now like a symbol of the nightmare, I was just some weird kind of hooker, a spectacle after the spectacle, reserved for a few spectators who had danced a conga with their tee shirts furled around their necks or their waists. But for you I was a princess on the Gran Avenida, shattered now by wind and fear (so that in your mind the avenue has become a time tunnel), the trophy reserved specially for you after a night of collective magic. For the police I will be a blank page. No one will ever understand my words of love. And you, Max, do you remember anything I said while you were screwing me?"

(The guy moves his head, clearly signaling assent, and his moist eyes, his tense shoulders, his stomach, his legs that jerk and jerk whenever she looks away, struggling to get free, his throbbing jugular, all say yes.)

"Do you remember I said *the wind*? Do you remember I said *the underground streets*? Do you remember I said *you are the photograph*? No, you really don't remember, do you? You were too drunk and too busy with my tits and my ass. And you had no idea, otherwise at the first opportunity you'd have been out of here like a shot. You'd like to get out of here now, wouldn't you, Max? Your image, your double, running across the garden, jumping over the fence, disappearing up the street, striding away like a middle distance runner, still half undressed, humming one of your hymns to bolster your courage, and then, after running for twenty minutes, turning up breathless in the bar where the rest of your group or club or squad or gang or whatever it's called are waiting for you, drinking a mug of beer and saying, Guys you're never going to believe what happened to me, I nearly got killed, some fucking whore from the suburbs, from the far side of the city and time, a whore from the fucking beyond who saw me on TV (we were on TV!) and took me home on her motorbike and sucked my dick and spread her legs for me and said words that were mysterious at first but then I understood them, no, I felt them, this whore said words I could feel in my liver and my balls, at first they sounded innocent or like she was hot for me or moaning because I was nailing her hard, but the thing is, guys, after a while they didn't sound so innocent, what I mean is, she didn't stop murmuring or whispering while I rode her, and that's normal, isn't it, but this wasn't normal, there was nothing normal about it, a whore who whispers while she's being fucked, OK, but then I heard what she was saying, I heard her fucking words plowing like a boat through a sea of testosterone, and I'm telling you guys, that supernatural voice made the sea of semen shudder and shrink away, the sea disappeared, leaving the sea floor exposed and the coast all dry, just stones and mountains, cliffs, ranges, dark crevices moist with fear, the boat sailing on over that emptiness, and I saw it with my own two eyes, my own three eyes, and I said, It's all right, it's all right, honey, shitting myself, petrified, and then I stood up, trying to look normal, all jittery but trying to hide it, and said I was going to the bathroom to siphon the python or take a dump, and she looked at me like I'd re-cited John fucking Donne, guys, or Ovid or something, and I walked backward keeping my eyes on her, still seeing that boat sailing on imperturbably through a sea of nothingness and electricity, as if planet Earth was being reborn and I was the only witness to its birth, but who was I witnessing for, the stars I guess, and when I got to the corridor, beyond the range of her gaze and her desire, instead of opening the bathroom door, I crept to the front door and crossed the garden, saying a silent prayer, and jumped the wall and started running up the street like the last runner from Marathon, bringing news not of victory but of defeat, the runner nobody listens to or congratulates or greets with a bowl of water, but he gets there alive, guys, and learns his lesson: Don't enter that castle, Don't follow that path, Don't venture into that territory. Even if you're singled out. Even if everything is against you."

(The guy nods his head. It's clear that he wants to express his agreement. The effort is making his face redden noticeably; his veins are swelling, his eyes are bulging.)

"But you didn't listen to my words, you couldn't distinguish them from my moaning, those last words, which might have saved you. I chose you well. Television doesn't lie, that's its only virtue (that and the old movies they show in the small hours of the morning), and the sight of your face, against the wire fence, after the conga that everyone cheered, prefigured (and hastened) the inevitable ending. I brought you home on my motorbike, I took off your clothes, I left you unconscious, I tied your hands and feet to an old chair, I put a sticking plaster over your mouth, not because I'm scared that your cries might alert someone, but because I don't want to hear you beg, I don't want to hear your pathetic stuttering apologies, your weak insistence that you're not like that, that it was all a game, that I've got it all wrong. Maybe I've got it all wrong. Maybe it's all a game. Maybe you're not like that. But the thing is, Max, no one's like that. I wasn't like that either. I'm not going to tell you about my pain, it's not as if you caused it; on the contrary, you gave me an orgasm. You were the lost prince who gave me an orgasm; you can be proud of yourself. And I gave you an opportunity to escape, but you were also the deaf prince. Now it's too late, it's getting light; your legs must be numb and cramped, your wrists are swollen; you shouldn't have struggled so much, I warned you when we started, Max, this was bound to happen. You'll have to make the best of it. Now is not the time for crying, or remembering conga lines, threats or beatings; it's time to look inside yourself and try to understand that sometimes, unexpectedly, people just walk away. You're naked in my chamber of horrors, Max, and your eyes are following my knife as it swings, as if it were the pendulum of a cuckoo clock. Close your eyes, Max, there's no need to go on looking; think of something nice, think of it as hard as you can . . ."

(His eyes, instead of closing, open wildly, and all his muscles wrench in one last desperate effort: the shock is so violent that the chair to which he is securely tied falls over. He hits his head and his hip on the ground, he loses control of his anal sphincter and bladder; he is seized by spasms; dust and filth from the flagstones stick to his wet skin.)

"I'm not going to pick you up, Max, you're fine like that. Keep your eyes open or close them, it doesn't matter; think of something nice or don't think at all. It's getting light out but, the way things are, it might just as well be getting dark. You're the prince and you're arriving at exactly the right time. You're welcome whenever you come and wherever you come from, whether you've come on a motorbike or on foot, whether or not you know what awaits you, whether you were tricked or came knowing that you would meet your destiny here. Your face, which until recently could express only stupidity or rage or hatred, is reconfigured now and can express what can only be guessed at inside a tunnel where physical time and verbal time flow into one another and mingle. You proceed resolutely through the corridors of my palace, barely pausing for the few seconds it takes to look at the pictures of the Catholic Monarchs, to drink a glass of crystal-clear water, to touch the mirrors' quicksilver with your fingertips. The castle only seems to be quiet, Max. Sometimes you think you're alone, but deep down you know that you're not. Your hand raised in salute, your naked torso, the tee-shirt furled around your waist, your warrior hymns about purity and the future, you leave all that behind. This castle is your mountain, and you will have to spend all your strength climbing and exploring it, because after that there will be nothing more; the mountain and the climbing will demand the highest price you can pay. Now think about what you're leaving, what you could and had to leave behind, and think about chance, the greatest criminal that ever walked the earth. Free yourself of fear and regret, Max, because you are already inside the castle, and here there is only the movement that will bring you ineluctably to my arms. Now you are inside the castle and you hear the doors closing behind you. Deep in the dream you walk on through passages and rooms of bare stone. What weapons do you carry, Max? Only your solitude. You know that somewhere I am waiting for you. You know that I am naked too. Sometimes you feel my tears, you see my tears flow on the dark stone and you think you have found me, but the room is empty, which distresses and yet at the same time excites you. Keep climbing, Max. The next room is dirty and doesn't seem to belong in a castle. There's an old TV that doesn't work and a folding bed with two mattresses on it. Someone is crying somewhere. You see children's drawings, old clothes covered with mold, dried blood and dust. You open another door. You call someone. You tell them not to cry. Your footsteps show in the dust on the floor of the passage. The tears sometimes seem to be dripping from the ceiling. It doesn't matter. The way things are, they might as well be spurting out the end of your dick. Sometimes all the rooms seem the same, the same room devastated by time. If you look at the ceiling you'll imagine you can see a star or a comet or a cuckoo clock sailing through the space that separates the prince's lips from those of the princess. Sometimes it all goes back to the way it used to be. The castle is dark, enormous, cold, and you are alone. But you know there is another person hidden somewhere, you feel the tears, you feel the nakedness. Peace and warmth are waiting for you in that person's arms, so you keep going, drawn on by hope, stepping around boxes full of memories that no one will ever look at again, suitcases full of old clothes that someone forgot or didn't want to throw away, and from time to time you call her, your princess—where is she?— your body stiff with cold, your teeth chattering, right in the middle of the tunnel, smiling in the darkness, free of fear for the first time perhaps, and with no intention of inspiring fear, spirited, exultant, full of life, feeling your way through the dark, opening doors, following passages that bring you closer to the tears, in the dark, guided only by your body's need for another body, falling down and getting up again, and finally you arrive at the central chamber, and finally you see me and cry out. I remain silent and cannot tell the nature of your cry. All I know is that we have finally come together, that you are the zealous prince and I am the princess without pity."

THE RETURN

I have good news and bad news. The good news is that there is life (of a kind) after this life. The bad news is that Jean-Claude Villeneuve is a necrophiliac.

Death caught up with me in a Paris disco at four in the morning. My doctor had warned me, but some things are stronger than reason. I was convinced, mistakenly (and even now it's something I regret), that drinking and dancing were not the most hazardous of my passions. Another reason I kept going out every night to the fashionable places in Paris was my routine as a middle manager at Fracsa; I was after what I couldn't find at work or in what people call the inner life: the buzz that you get from a certain excess.

But I'd rather not talk about that, or only as much as I have to. When my death occurred, I was recently divorced and thirty-four years old. I hardly realized what was going on. A sudden sharp pain in the chest, her face, the face of Cécile Lamballe, the woman of my dreams, imperturbable as ever, the dance floor spinning in a brutal whirl, sucking in the dancers and the shadows, and then a brief moment of darkness.

What happened next was like what you sometimes see in movies and I'd like to say a few words about that.

In life I wasn't especially intelligent. I'm still not (though I've learned a lot). When I say intelligent, what I really mean is thoughtful. But I have a certain energy and a certain taste. What I mean is, I'm not a philistine. It couldn't be said, objectively, that I'd ever behaved like a philistine. It's true that I graduated in business studies, but that didn't stop me from reading a good book or seeing a play every now and then, or being a keener moviegoer than most. Some of the movies I was pressured to see by my ex-wife. But the others I saw for love of the seventh art.

Like just about everyone else, I went to see *Ghost*, I don't know if you remember it, a box office hit, with Demi Moore and Whoopi Goldberg, the one where Patrick Swayze gets killed and his body is left lying on a Manhattan street, or in an alley, maybe, on a dirty pavement anyway, while in a special-effects extravaganza (they were special for the time, anyway) his soul comes out of his body and stares at it in astonishment. Well, apart from the special effects, I thought it was idiotic. A typical Hollywood cop-out, inane and unbelievable.

But when my turn came, that was exactly what happened. I was stunned. First, because I had died, which always comes as a surprise, except, I guess, in some cases of suicide, and then because I was unwillingly acting out one of the worst scenes of *Ghost*. One of the many things experience has taught me is that there is sometimes more to American naiveté than meets the eye; it can hide something that we Europeans can't or don't want to understand. But once I was dead, I didn't care about that. Once I was dead, I felt like bursting out laughing.

You get used to anything in the end, but in the early hours of that morning I felt dizzy or drunk, not because I was under the influence of alcohol on the night of my death—I wasn't;

on the contrary, it had been a night of pineapple juice and non-alcoholic beer—but because of the shock of being dead, the fear of being dead and not knowing what was coming next. When you die the real world *shifts* slightly and that adds to the dizziness. It's as if you'd suddenly put on a pair of glasses that don't match your prescription; they're not all that different, but not quite right. And the worst thing is you know that the glasses you've put on belong to you and nobody else. And the real world shifts slightly to the right, down a little, the distance separating you from a given object changes almost imperceptibly, but you perceive that change as an abyss, and the abyss adds to your dizziness, but in the end it doesn't matter.

It makes you want to cry or pray. The first minutes of ghosthood are minutes of imminent knockout. You're like a punch-drunk boxer staggering around the ring in the drawn-out moment of the ring's evaporation. But then you calm down and what generally happens is that you follow the people who were there when you died—your girlfriend, your friends—or you follow your own body.

I was with Cécile Lamballe, the woman of my dreams, I was with her and saw her just before I died, but when my soul came out of my body I couldn't see her anywhere. It was quite a surprise and a great disappointment, especially when I think about it now, though back then I didn't have time to be sad. There I was, looking at my body lying in a grotesque heap on the floor, as if, seized by the dance and the heart attack, I'd completely fallen apart, or as if I hadn't died of a heart attack at all but dropped from the top of a skyscraper, and while I looked on and walked around and fell over (because I was completely dizzy), a volunteer (there's always someone) gave me (or my body) mouth-to-mouth, while another one thumped my chest, then someone thought of switching off the music and a murmur of disapproval swept through the disco, which was pretty full in spite of the late hour, and the deep voice of a waiter or a security guard told them all not to touch me, to wait for the police and the magistrate, and although I was groggy I would have liked to say, Keep going, keep trying to revive me, but they were tired, and as soon as the police were mentioned they all stepped back, and my body lay there on its own at the edge of the dance floor, eyes closed, until a charitable soul put a blanket over me to cover what was now definitively dead.

Then the police turned up along with some guys who confirmed what everyone already knew, and later the magistrate arrived and only then did I realize that Cécile Lamballe had vanished from the disco, so when they picked up my body and put it in an ambulance, I followed the medics and slipped into the back of the vehicle, and off I went with them into the sad and weary Paris dawn.

What a paltry thing it seemed, my body or my ex-body (I'm not sure how to put it), confronted with the labyrinthine bureaucracy of death. First they took me to the basement of a hospital, although I couldn't swear it was a hospital, where a young woman with glasses ordered them to undress me, and when they left her on her own, she spent a few moments examining and touching me. Then they covered me with a sheet, and moved me to another room to take a complete set of fingerprints. Then they brought me back to the first room, which was empty now, and I stayed there for what seemed like a long time, though I couldn't say how many hours. Maybe it was only minutes, but I was getting more and more bored.

After a while, a black orderly came to get me and take me
to another underground room, where he handed me over to
a pair of young guys also dressed in white, who made me feel
uneasy right from the start, I don't know why. Maybe it was
their would-be sophisticated way of talking, which identified
them as a pair of tenth-rate artists, maybe it was their earrings, the sort all the hipsters were wearing that season in the
discos that I had frequented with an irresponsible persistence:
hexagonal in shape and somehow evocative of runaways from
a fantastic bestiary.

The new orderlies made some notes in a book, spoke with
the black guy for a few minutes (I don't know what that was
about) and then the black guy went and left us alone. So in
the room there were the two young guys behind the desk, fill-
ing out forms and chatting away, there was my body on the
trolley, covered from head to foot, and me standing beside it,
with my left hand resting on the trolley's metal edge, trying
to think with a modicum of clarity about what the days to
come might hold, if there were any days to come, which was
far from obvious to me right then.

Then one of the young guys approached the trolley and
uncovered me, or uncovered my body, and scrutinized it for
a few seconds with a thoughtful expression that didn't bode
well. After a while he covered it up again, and the two of them
wheeled the trolley into the next room, a sort of freezing hon-
eycomb, which I soon discovered was a storehouse for corpses.
I would never have imagined that so many people could die
in the course of an ordinary night in Paris. They slid my body
into a refrigerated niche and left. I didn't follow them.

I spent that whole day there in the morgue. Every so often I went to the door, which had a little glass window, and

checked the time on the wall clock in the next room. The feeling of dizziness gradually abated, although at one point I got to thinking about heaven and hell, reward and punishment, and I had a panic attack, but that bout of irrational fear was soon over. And, in fact, I was starting to feel better.

Throughout the day new bodies kept arriving, but never accompanied by ghosts, and at about four in the afternoon, a near-sighted young man performed an autopsy on me and established the causes of my accidental death. I have to admit I didn't have the stomach to watch them open me up. But I went to the autopsy room and listened as the coroner and his assistant, quite a pretty girl, performed their task efficiently and quickly—if only all public servants worked like that—while I waited with my back turned, looking at the ivory-colored tiles on the wall. Then they washed me and sewed me up and an orderly took me back to the morgue again.

I stayed there until eleven at night, sitting on the floor in front of my refrigerated niche, and although at one point I thought I was going to doze off, I was beyond the need for sleep, so what I did was just go on thinking about my past life and the enigmatic future (to give it a name of some kind) that lay before me. After ten o'clock, the comings and goings, which during the day had been like a constant but barely perceptible dripping, stopped or diminished considerably. At five past eleven the young guys with the hexagonal earrings reappeared. I was startled when they opened the door. But I was beginning to get used to my ghostly state and, having recognized them, I remained seated on the floor, thinking of the distance separating me from Cécile Lamballe, which was infinitely greater than the distance between us when I was still alive. Realizations always come too late. In life I was afraid of being a toy (or less than a toy) for Cécile, and now that I was dead, that fate, once the cause of my insomnia and pervasive insecurity, seemed sweet, and not without a certain grace and substance: the solidity of the real.

But I was talking about the hipster orderlies. I saw them come into the morgue and although I noticed something cautious in their bearing, which sat oddly with their oily, feline manner, like wannabe artists out clubbing, at first I paid no attention to their movements and their whispering until one of them opened the niche where my body was lying.

Then I got up and started watching them. Moving like seasoned professionals, they placed my body on a trolley. Then they rolled the trolley out of the morgue and along a long corridor, sloping gently upwards, which eventually led into the building's parking garage. For a moment I thought they were stealing my body. In my delirium I imagined Cécile Lamballe, the milk-white face of Cécile Lamballe; I imagined her emerging from the darkness of the parking lot to give the pseudo-artists the sum they had demanded for the rescue of my body. But there was no one in the garage—clearly, I was still a long way from recovering my powers of reasoning or even my composure.

To tell the truth I'd been really hoping for a quiet night.

For a few moments, as I followed the orderlies between the unwelcoming rows of cars with a certain trepidation and disquiet, I experienced the dizziness I had felt in my first few minutes as a ghost. They put my body in the trunk of a gray Renault, covered all over with little dents, and we emerged from the belly of that building, which I was already beginning to think of as home, into the utter freedom of the Paris night.

I can't remember now which avenues and streets we took.

The orderlies were high, as I was able to ascertain from closer observation, and they were talking about people well beyond their social reach. My first impression was soon confirmed: they were pathetic losers, but there was something in their attitude, something, I thought at first, like hope, and then it seemed like innocence, which made me feel close to them somehow. Deep down, we were similar, not then and not in the moments leading up to my death, but they were similar to how I imagined myself at twenty-two or twenty-five, when I was still a student and still believed that one day the world was going to fall at my feet.

The Renault pulled up in front of a mansion in one of the most exclusive neighborhoods of Paris. That's how it seemed to me, anyway. One of the pseudo-artists got out of the car and rang a bell. After a while, a voice from the darkness told him to move, no, *suggested* that he move a little to the right and lift his chin. The orderly did as he was told and lifted his head. The other one looked out the window of the car and waved in the direction of a television camera that was observing us from the top of the gate. The voice made a throat-clearing sound (at that point I *knew* that I would soon meet a man of the utmost reserve) and said that we could enter.

Straightaway the gate opened with a faint squeaking sound and the car drove in along a paved drive that snaked through a garden full of trees and shrubs, with a slightly overgrown look that owed more to whim than to neglect. We stopped beside one of the wings of the house. While the orderlies were removing my body from the trunk, I looked at the building in dismay and awe. Never in all my life had I been inside a house like that. It looked old. It must have been worth a fortune. I couldn't say any more without stretching my knowledge of architecture.

We went in through one of the service entrances. We crossed the kitchen, which was spotless and cold like the kitchen in a restaurant that has been closed for many years, and then we followed a dim corridor at the end of which we took an elevator down to the basement. When the doors of the elevator opened, there was Jean-Claude Villeneuve. I recognized him immediately. The long white hair, the thick glasses, the gray gaze that seemed to belong to a helpless child, while the firm narrow lips denoted, on the contrary, a man who knew very well what he wanted. He was wearing jeans and a white, short-sleeved shirt. I was shocked, because in the photos of Villeneuve that I had seen, his clothes had always been elegant. Discreet, yes, but elegant. The Villeneuve before me now, by contrast, looked like an old rock star suffering from insomnia. His gait, however, was unmistakable; he moved with the same unsteadiness that I had seen so often on television, when he stepped up onto the catwalk at the end of his autumn-winter or spring-summer shows, almost as if it was a chore, hauled out by his favorite models to receive the public's unanimous applause.

The orderlies put my body on a dark green sofa and took a few steps back, waiting for Villeneuve's verdict. He approached my body, uncovered my face, and then without saying a word went over to a little desk made (I assume) of fine wood, from which he extracted an envelope. The orderlies took the envelope, which almost certainly contained a considerable sum of cash, though neither of them bothered to count it, and then one of them said that they would come back at seven the next morning to pick me up, and they left. Villeneueve ignored his parting words. The orderlies went out the way we'd come in; I heard the sound of the elevator and then silence. Paying no attention to my body, Villeneuve switched on a television monitor. I looked over his shoulder. The pseudo-artists were at the gate, waiting for Villeneuve to let them out. Then the car drove off into the streets of that highly exclusive neighborhood and the metal gate shut with a brief squeaking noise.

From that moment on, everything in my new supernatural life began to change, in accelerating phases that were perfectly distinct from each other, in spite of their rapid succession. Villeneuve went over to what looked like a standard hotel minibar and took out an apple juice. He removed the cap, began to drink straight from the bottle and switched off the security monitor. As he drank, he put on some music. Music I had never heard, or maybe I had, but when I listened carefully it didn't seem familiar: electric guitars, a piano, a saxophone, a sorrowful and melancholic piece, but strong as well, as if the composer's spirit was determined not to yield. I went over to the stereo hoping to see the name on the cover of the CD but I couldn't see anything. Only Villeneuve's face, which looked strange in the semi-darkness, as if being on his own again and drinking the apple juice had given him a hot flush. I noticed a drop of sweat in the middle of his cheek. A tiny drop rolling slowly down toward his chin. I also thought I could see him trembling slightly.

Then Villeneuve put the glass down beside the CD player and approached my body. For a while he looked at me as if he didn't know what to do, though he did, or as if he was attempting to guess what hopes and desires had once agitated the contents of that plastic body bag, which were now at his disposal. He stayed like that for some time. I didn't know what his intentions were—I've always been an innocent. If I'd known, I would have been nervous. But I didn't, so I sat down in one of the comfortable leather armchairs in the room and waited.

With extreme care, Villeneuve unwrapped the parcel containing my body, rucking the bag up under my legs, and then (after two or three endless minutes) he removed it entirely and left my corpse naked on the sofa, which was upholstered with green leather. He stood up straightaway—he'd been kneeling—took off his shirt and paused, but keeping his eyes on me, and that was when I stood up too, came a little closer and saw my naked body, slightly fatter than I would have liked, but not too bad—eyes closed, an absent expression on my face—and I saw Villeneuve's torso, a sight very few people have seen, since the great designer is renowned for his discretion among many other qualities (the press, for example, has never published photos of him at the beach), and I tried to read his expression and guess what would happen next, but all I could see in his face was diffidence; he looked more diffident than in the photos, *infinitely* more diffident in fact than he looked in the photos in the fashion and gossip magazines.

Villeneuve removed his trousers and socks and lay down beside my body. Well, at that point I *did* realize what was going on, and I was dumbstruck. It's easy enough to imagine what came next, but it wasn't what you'd call bacchanalian. Villeneuve hugged me, caressed me, kissed me chastely on the lips. He massaged my penis and testicles with something of the delicacy once lavished on me by Cécile Lamballe, the woman of my dreams, and after a quarter of an hour of cuddling in the semi-darkness I noticed that he had an erection. My god, I thought, now he's going to sodomize me. But that's not what happened. To my surprise, the designer rubbed himself against one of my thighs till he came. I would have liked to shut my eyes at that point but I couldn't. My reactions were contradictory; I felt disgusted by what I was seeing, grateful for not having been sodomized, surprised to discover Villeneuve's secret, angry at the orderlies for having rented out my body, and even flattered to have served, unwillingly, as an object of desire for one of the most famous men in France.

After coming, Villeneuve closed his eyes and sighed. In that sigh I thought I could detect a hint of disgust. He sat up quickly and stayed there on the sofa with his back to my body for a few seconds, while he wiped his dripping member with his hand. You should be ashamed, I said.

It was the first time I'd spoken since my death. Villeneuve raised his head, quite unsurprised, or at any rate much less surprised than I would have been in his situation, while reaching down with one hand to feel for his glasses on the carpet.

I knew at once that he had heard me. It seemed like a miracle. Suddenly I felt so happy that I forgave him his act of depravity. And yet, like an idiot, I repeated: You should be ashamed. Who's there? said Villeneuve. It's me, I said, the ghost of the body you just raped. Villeneuve went pale, and then, almost simultaneously, a blush rose in his cheeks. I was worried that he would have a heart attack or die of fright, although to tell the truth he didn't look all that frightened.

It's not a problem, I said in a conciliatory tone, You're forgiven.

Villeneuve switched on the light and looked in all the corners of the room. I thought he'd gone crazy, because there was clearly no one else there; only a pygmy could have hidden in that room, not even a pygmy, a gnome. But then I realized that, far from being crazy, the designer was displaying nerves of steel: he wasn't looking for a person but a speaker. As I calmed down, I felt a surge of sympathy for him. There was something admirable about his methodical way of searching the room. Me, I'd have been out of there like a shot.

I'm no speaker, I said. Nor am I a video camera. Please, try to calm down; take a seat and we can talk. And most of all, don't be afraid of me. I'm not going to do anything to you. That's what I said; then I kept quiet and watched Villeneuve, who barely hesitated before continuing his search. I let him go ahead. While he messed up the room, I remained seated in one of the comfortable armchairs. Then I had an idea. I suggested that we shut ourselves in a small room (as small as a coffin were my exact words), where no speakers or cameras could possibly have been planted, and I could go on talking to him there and convince him to accept my nature, my new nature, that is. But while he was considering my proposal, it occurred to me that I hadn't expressed myself very well, since my ghostly state could not be called, in any sense, a "nature." My nature, however you looked at it, was still that of a living being. And yet it was clear that I was not alive. The thought crossed my mind that it might all be a dream. Summoning some ghostly courage, I told myself that if it was a dream, the best (and the only) thing I could do was to go on dreaming. From experience I know that trying to wrench yourself out of a nightmare is futile and simply adds pain to pain or terror to terror.

So I repeated my proposal, and this time Villeneuve stopped searching and froze (I examined his face, which I'd seen so often in the glossy magazines, and saw the same expression, a solitary, elegant expression, although now there were a few telltale drops of sweat rolling down his forehead and his cheeks). He left the room. I followed him. Halfway down a long corridor, he stopped and said: Are you still with me? His voice was strangely appealing, rich in tones that seemed to be converging on a genuine warmth, though perhaps it was just an illusion.

I'm here, I said.

Villeneuve moved his head in a way I couldn't interpret and continued to wander through his house, stopping in each room and on each landing to ask if I was still with him, a question to which I replied without fail, trying to make my voice sound relaxed, or at least trying to give it a singular tone (in life it was always an ordinary, run-of-the-mill sort of voice), no doubt influenced by the reedy (sometimes almost whistle-like) yet extremely distinguished voice of the designer. To each reply I also added details about the place where we happened to be, with the aim of achieving greater credibility; for example, if there was a lamp with a tobacco-colored shade and a wrought iron stand, I said so. I'm still here, next to you, and now we're in a room where the only source of light is a lamp with a tobacco-colored shade and a wrought iron stand. And Villeneuve said yes or corrected me—That's cast iron—but his eyes were fixed on the ground as he spoke, as if he was afraid that I might suddenly materialize, or didn't want to embarrass me, and I'd say: Sorry, I didn't notice, or: That's what I meant. And Villeneuve moved his head ambivalently, as if accepting my excuses or just getting a clearer idea of the ghost he had to deal with.

And so we went all around the house, and as we moved from place to place, Villeneuve grew or seemed to grow calmer, while I became more nervous, because I've never been much good at describing things, especially if they're not objects in everyday use, or if they happen to be paintings no doubt worth a fortune by contemporary artists I know absolutely nothing about, or sculptures that Villeneuve had collected in the course of his travels (incognito) all around the world.

And so on, until we came to a little room, covered inside with a layer of cement, in which there was nothing, not one piece of furniture, not a single light, and we shut ourselves in that room, in the dark. An embarrassing situation, on the face of it, but for me it was like a second or a third birth; that is, it was like hope beginning and with it the desperate aware-ness of hope. Villeneuve said: Describe the place where we are now. And I said that it was like death, not like real death but death as we imagine it when we're alive. And Villeneuve said: Describe it. Everything is dark, I said. It's like a nuclear bomb shelter. And I added that in a place like that the soul contracts, and I would have gone on spelling out what I felt, the void that had come to inhabit my soul long before I died and of which I'd been unaware until then, but Villeneuve cut me off me, saying, That's enough, he believed me, and sud-denly he opened the door.

I followed him to the main living room, where he poured himself a whiskey and proceeded, in a few well-measured sen-tences, to ask me to forgive him for what he had done with my body. You're forgiven, I said. I'm open-minded. To be honest, I'm not sure I know what being open-minded means, but I felt it was my duty to wipe the slate clean and clear our future relationship of any guilt or resentment.

You must be wondering why I do what I do, said Villeneuve.

I assured him that I had no intention of asking for an explanation. Nevertheless, Villeneuve insisted on giving me one. With anyone else, it would have become a very unpleas-ant evening, but I was listening to Jean-Claude Villeneuve, the greatest designer in France, which is to say the world, and time flew as I was given a brief account of his childhood and teenage years, his youth, his reservations about sex, his experiences with a number of men, and with a number of women, his solitary habits, his morbid dread of harming anyone which may have been a screen to hide his dread of being harmed, his artistic tastes, which I admired (and envied) unreservedly, his chronic insecurity, his conflicts with a number of famous designers, his first jobs for a fashion house, his voyages of initiation, which he declined to recount in detail, his friendships with three of Europe's finest screen actresses, his association with the pair of pseudo-artists from the morgue, who from time to time provided him with corpses, with which he spent only one night, his fragility, which he compared to an endless demolition in slow motion, and so on, until the first light of dawn began to filter through the curtains of the living room and Villeneuve brought his long exposé to a close.

We remained silent for a long time. I knew that both of us were, if not overwhelmed with joy, at least reasonably happy.

Before long the orderlies arrived. Villeneuve looked at the floor and asked me what he should do. After all, the body they had come for was mine. I thanked him for his thoughtfulness but also assured him that I was now beyond caring about such things. Do what you normally do, I said. Will you go? he asked. I had already made up my mind, and yet I pretended to think for a few seconds before saying no, I wasn't going to leave. If he didn't mind, of course. Villeneuve seemed relieved: I don't mind, on the contrary, he said. Then a bell rang, and Villeneuve switched on the monitors and opened the gates for the rent-a-corpse guys, who came in without saying a word.

Exhausted by the night's events, Villeneuve didn't get up from the sofa. The pseudo-artists greeted him, and it seemed to me that one of them was in the mood for a chat, but the other one gave him a nudge and they went down to get my body without further ado. Villeneuve had his eyes closed and seemed to be asleep. I followed the orderlies down to the basement. My body was lying there half covered by the body bag from the morgue. I watched them put it back in the bag and carry it up and place it in the trunk of the car. I imagined it waiting there, in the cold morgue, until a relative or my ex-wife came to claim it. But I mustn't give in to sentimentality, I thought, and when the orderlies' car left the garden and vanished down that elegant, tree-lined street, I didn't feel the slightest twinge of nostalgia or sadness or melancholy.

When I returned to the living room, Villeneuve was still on the sofa, with his arms crossed, shivering with cold, and he was talking to himself (though I soon realized that he thought he was talking to me). I sat on a chair in front of him, a chair of carved wood with a satin backrest, facing the window and the garden and the beautiful morning light, and I let him go on talking as long as he liked.

BUBA

for Juan Villoro

The city of sanity. The city of common sense. That's what the people of Barcelona used to call their city. I liked it. It was a beautiful city and I think I felt at home there from the second day on (if I said from the very first day I'd be exaggerating) but the club wasn't doing so well, and people started going kind of sour, it always happens, I'm speaking from experience, at first the fans want your autograph, they hang around outside the hotel, they're so friendly it's exhausting, but then you have a run of bad luck, which leads to another, and soon enough they start making faces, maybe you're just lazy, they think, or partying too much, or whoring, you know what I mean, people start to take an interest in what you're getting paid, they speculate, they calculate, and there's always a wise guy who'll come out and accuse you of being a thief or something a thousand times worse. This stuff happens everywhere, I'd already been through it once, but that was back home, in my country, and this time I was a foreigner, and the press and the fans always expect something extra special from foreigners. I mean, why else would they hire us?

Me, for example, I'm a left winger, everyone knows that.

When I played in Latin America (in Chile, then in Argentina) I scored an average of ten goals per season. But my debut here was disastrous; I got injured in the third game, had to have an operation on my ligaments, and my recovery, which in theory should have been quick, was laborious and drawn-out, but I won't go into that. Suddenly I was back to feeling as lonely as a lighthouse. That's the way it was. I spent a fortune on calls to Santiago, but that only made Mom and Dad worry; they didn't understand at all. So one day I decided to go whoring. Why should I deny it? That's the way it was. Actually, I was just following some advice that Cerrone, the Argentinean goalkeeper, had given me one day. He said to me, Kid, if you can't think of anything else to do, and your problems are eating away at you, go see a whore. He was great guy, Cerrone. I would have been nineteen at the most and I had just joined Gimnasia y Esgrima in La Plata. Cerrone was already around 35 or 40, his age was a mystery, and he was the only one of the older players who wasn't married. Some said Cerrone was queer. That made me wary of him for a start. I was a shy sort of kid and I thought that if I got to know a homosexual, he'd try and get me into bed straightway. Anyway, maybe he was, maybe he wasn't, all I know for sure is that one afternoon, when I was lower than ever, he took me aside, it was the first time we'd talked, really, and said he was going to take me to meet some girls from Buenos Aires. I'll never forget that night. The apartment was downtown, and while Cerrone stayed in the living room drinking and watching a late show on TV, I slept with an Argentinean woman for the first time, and my depression began to lift. Going home the next morning, I knew that things would get better and that I still had plenty of glory days to look forward to in the Argentinean

League. I was bound to get depressed occasionally, I thought, but Cerrone had given me the remedy to make it bearable.

And I did the same thing at my first European club: I went whoring and it helped me to get over the injury, the recovery period and the loneliness. Did it become a habit? Maybe, maybe not; that's not something I can really judge objectively. The whores there are gorgeous, the high-class whores I mean, and most of them are pretty smart and educated too, so it really isn't difficult to develop a serious taste for them.

Anyhow, I started going out every night, even Sundays when there was a match on, and the injured players were expected to be there, in the stands, doing their bit as VIP supporters. But that doesn't help your injuries to heal, and I preferred to spend Sunday afternoons in some massage parlor with a glass of whiskey and one or two lady friends on either side, discussing more serious matters. At first, of course, no one realized. I wasn't the only injured player, there must have been six or seven of us in the dry dock—bad luck seemed to be dogging the club. But of course, there's always some fucking journalist who sees you coming out of a nightclub at four in the morning, and the game's up. News travels fast in Barcelona, though it seems such a big and civilized city. Soccer news, I mean.

One morning the trainer called and said he'd found out about the life I was leading: it was inappropriate for a professional athlete and had to stop. Naturally I said, Yes, I'd just been having a bit of fun, and then I went on like before, because, come on, what else was I going to do while I was still unfit to play and the team slid down the ranking and opening the paper on a Monday morning to look at the league table was a downer week after week. Also, I was convinced that what had worked for me in Argentina was going to work for me in Spain, and the worst thing was, I was right: it did work. But then the bureaucrats got involved and told me: Listen, Acevedo, this has got to stop, you're becoming a bad example for the young and a disastrous investment for the club, we only employ hard workers here, so from now on, no more nightlife, or else. And then, before I knew it, I was liable for a fine if I broke the curfew; I could have paid it, of course, but if I was going to be throwing money away, I'd rather have sent it to someone in Chile, like my uncle Julio, so he could fix up his house.

These things happen and you have to deal with it. So I dealt with it and resolved to go out less often, once every two weeks, say, but then Buba turned up and the management decided that the best thing for me would be to move out of the hotel and share the apartment they'd rented for him right next to our training ground; it was small but kind of cozy, with two bedrooms and a terrace that was tiny but had a good view. So that was what I had to do. I packed my bags and went to the apartment with one of the club's administrators, and since Buba wasn't there, I chose the bedroom I wanted and took out my stuff and put it in the closet, and then the administrator gave me my keys and left and I lay down to take a siesta.

It was about five, and earlier that afternoon I'd put away a *fideuà*, a Barcelona specialty, which I'd already tried (I love it, but it isn't easy to digest) and as soon as I flopped onto my new bed I felt so tired it was all I could do to pull off my shoes before I fell asleep. Then I had the weirdest dream. I dreamed I was in Santiago again, in my neighborhood, La Cisterna, and I was with my father, crossing the square where there's a statue of Che Guevara, the first statue of Che in the Americas, outside Cuba, and that was what my father was telling me in the dream, the story of the statue and the various attempts to destroy it before the soldiers came and blew it away, and as we walked I was looking all around and it was like we were deep in the jungle, and my father was saying the statue should be around here somewhere, but you couldn't see anything, the grass was high and only a few feeble rays of sunlight were filtering down through the trees, just enough to see by, to show that it was daytime, and we were following a path of earth and stones, but the vegetation on either side was dense, there were even lianas, and you couldn't see anything, only shadows, until suddenly we came to a sort of clearing, with forest all around, and then my father stopped, put one hand on my shoulder and pointed with the other hand to something rearing up in the middle of the clearing, a pedestal of light-colored cement, and on top of the pedestal there was nothing, not a trace of the statue of Che, but my father and I already knew that, Che had been removed from there a long time ago, it didn't come as a surprise, what mattered was that we were there together, my old man and me, and we had found the exact place where the statue used to stand before, but while we looked around the clearing, standing still, as if absorbed in our discovery, I noticed that there was something at the bottom of the pedestal, on the other side, something dark, which was moving, and I broke away from my father (he had been holding me by the hand) and began to walk slowly toward it.

Then I saw what it was: on the other side of the pedestal there was a black man, stark naked, drawing on the ground, and I knew straightaway that the black man was Buba, my teammate, my housemate, although to tell you the truth, like the rest of the players, I'd only ever seen Buba in a couple of photos, and when you've only glanced at someone's picture in the paper you can't have a clear idea of how they look. But it was Buba, I had no doubts about that. And then I thought: Fucking hell! I must be dreaming, I'm not in Chile, I'm not in La Cisterna, my father hasn't brought me to any square, and this jerk in his birthday suit isn't Buba, the African midfielder who just signed with our club.

Just as I came to the end of that train of thought, the black guy looked up and smiled at me, dropped the stick he'd been using to draw in the yellow earth (and it really was genuine Chilean earth), leaped to his feet and held out his hand. You're Acevedo, he said, glad to meet you, kid, that's what he said. And I thought: Maybe we're on tour? But where? In Chile? Impossible. And then we shook hands and Buba squeezed my hand hard and held onto it, and while he was squeezing my hand I looked down and saw the drawings on the earth, just scribbles, what else could they have been, but it was like I could join them up, if you see what I mean, and the scribbles made sense, that is, they weren't just scribbles, they were something more. Then I tried to bend down and get a closer look, but I couldn't because Buba's hand was gripping mine and when I tried to free myself (not so much to see the drawings anymore, but to get away from him, to put some distance between us, because I was starting to feel something like fear), I couldn't; Buba's hand and his arm seemed to be the hand and arm of a statue, a freshly cast statue, and my hand was embedded in that material, which felt like mud and then like molten lava.

I think that was when I woke up. I heard noises in the

kitchen and then steps going from the living room to the other bedroom, and my arm was numb (I'd fallen asleep in an awkward position, which happened quite often back then, while I was recovering from the injury), and I stayed in my bedroom waiting; the door was open, so he must have seen me; I waited and waited but he didn't come to the door. I heard his footsteps, I cleared my throat, coughed, stood up; then I heard someone opening the front door and shutting it again, very quietly. I spent the rest of the day alone, sitting in front of the TV, getting more and more nervous. I had a look in his room (I'm not a busybody but I couldn't help myself); he'd put his clothes in the closet drawers: track suits, some formal wear and some African robes that looked like fancy dress to me but actually they were beautiful. He'd laid out his toiletries in the bathroom: a straight-edge razor (I use disposable razors and hadn't seen a straight-edge for a while), lotion, English aftershave (or bought in England anyway), and a very large, earth-colored sponge in the bathtub.

Buba returned to our new home at nine o'clock that night. My eyes were hurting from watching so much TV, and he told me he'd come back from a session with the city's sportswriters. We didn't really hit it off at the start and it took us a while to become friends, though sometimes, thinking back, I come to the melancholy conclusion that we were never what you would really call friends. Other times, though, right now for example, I think we were pretty good friends, and one thing's for sure, anyway: if Buba had a friend in that club, it was me.

It's not like our life together was difficult. A woman came in twice a week to clean the apartment and we tidied up after ourselves, washed our own dishes, made our beds, you know, the usual deal. Sometimes I went out at night with Herrera, a local kid who'd come up through the ranks and ended up securing a place on the national team, and sometimes Buba came with us, but not very often, because he didn't really like going out. When I stayed home I'd watch TV and Buba would shut himself in his room and put on music. African music. At first I didn't like Buba's cassettes at all. In fact, the first time I heard them, the day after he moved in, I got a fright. I was watching a documentary about the Amazon, waiting for a Van Damme movie to begin, and all of a sudden it was like someone was being killed in Buba's room. Put yourself in my place. It's not every day you face something like that; it would have rattled anyone. What did I do? Well, I stood up, I had my back to Buba's door, and naturally I braced myself, but then I realized it was a tape, the shouts were coming from the cassette player. Then the noises died away, all you could hear was something like a drum, and then someone groaning, or weeping, gradually getting louder. I could only take so much. I remember walking to the door, rapping on it with my knuckles: no response. At that point I thought it was Buba weeping and groaning, not the cassette. But then I heard Buba's voice asking what I wanted and I didn't know what to say. It was all quite embarrassing. I asked him to turn it down. I tried as hard as I possibly could to make my voice sound normal. Buba was quiet for a while. Then the music stopped (by then it was just a drum beat really, with maybe some kind of flute as well) and Buba said he was going to sleep. Good night, I said and returned to the armchair, where I sat for a while watching the documentary about Amazon Indians with the sound off.

Otherwise, everyday life, as they say, was easy enough. Buba had just arrived and he still hadn't played a game with the first team. The club had a surplus of players at the time but there's no point going into that. In addition to the Spaniards, including four players from the national team, there was Antoine García the French sweeper, Delève the Belgian forward, Neuhuys the Dutch center-back, Jovanovic the Yugoslavian forward, plus the Argentinean Percutti and the Uruguayan Buzatti, who were midfielders. But things were going badly for us: after ten disastrous matches we were in the middle of the rankings and it looked like we were heading down. To tell the truth, I don't know why they signed Buba. I guess they did it to appease the fans, who were complaining more and more bitterly, but on the face of it, at least, they'd screwed up completely. Everyone was hoping they'd sign an emergency replacement for me, a winger, that is, not a midfielder, because we already had Percutti, but managers everywhere tend to be pretty stupid: they jumped at the first opportunity and that's how Buba ended up with us. Lots of people thought the plan was to get him to do a stint with the second team, which was way down in the second division B at the time, but Buba's agent said no way, the contract was perfectly clear: either Buba played with the first team or he didn't play at all. So there we were, the two of us, in our apartment near the training ground, him on the bench every Sunday, and me still recovering from the injury and sunk in that awful depression. And we were the two youngest players, like I told you already, and if I didn't I'm telling you now, although there was some speculation about that too for a while. I was twenty-two at the time, no doubt there. People said Buba was nineteen, though he looked more like he was twenty-nine, and naturally some smartass journalist claimed that our managers had been duped: in Buba's country birth certificates were issued à la carte, he said; Buba not only looked older but was older; in short, the deal had been a rip-off.

I didn't know what to think, really. In any case, living with Buba day by day wasn't hard at all. Sometimes he shut himself in his bedroom at night and put on his shouting and groaning music, but you get used to anything. Anyway I liked to watch TV with the sound up loud till the early hours of the morning, and as far as I know Buba never complained about that. At the start we had trouble communicating, because we didn't share a language, so we talked mainly with gestures. But then Buba learned some Spanish and some mornings at breakfast we even talked about movies, always a favorite topic of mine, though to tell the truth Buba wasn't very talkative, or very interested in movies, for that matter. In fact, now that I think of it, Buba was pretty quiet. It's not that he was shy or scared of putting his foot in it; Herrera, who could speak English, once told me it was just that he didn't have anything to say. Crazy Herrera. He was such a great guy. A good friend, too. We used to go out a lot, Herrera, Pepito Vila, who had come up from the juniors too, Buba and me. But Buba was always quiet, watching it all as if he was only half there, and although Herrera sometimes went out of his way to speak to him in English, and he spoke fluent English, Herrera, Buba would always go off on a tangent, as if he couldn't be bothered explaining stuff about his childhood and his country, and especially not about his family, to the point where Herrera was convinced that something bad must have happened to him when he was a kid, because he kept refusing to give away anything personal at all; it's like his village was razed, said Herrera, who was left-wing and still is, it's like he saw his parents and brothers and sisters killed right in front of him, and he's been trying to erase it from his mind all these years, which would have made sense if Herrera's assumptions had been correct, but in fact, and this is something I always knew or sensed, Herrera was wrong; the reason Buba didn't talk much was just that he wasn't very talkative, irrespective of whether his childhood and teenage years had been happy or traumatic: Buba's life was surrounded by mystery because that's how Buba was, simple as that.

But there was one thing we knew for sure: the team was in a bad way. Herrera and Buba looked like they'd be stuck on the bench till the end of the season, I was injured, and any provincial team could come and beat us on our home ground. Then, when it seemed like we'd hit rock bottom and nothing more could go wrong, Percutti got injured and the boss had no choice but to select Buba. I remember it like it was yesterday. We had to play on a Saturday, and at the Thursday training session, Percutti fucked up his knee in an accidental collision with the center back, Palau. So our trainer got Buba to take his place at Friday training and it was obvious to Herrera and me that he'd be selected for the Saturday match.

When we told him that afternoon, in the hotel where they were keeping us together (although we were playing at home against a theoretically weak opponent, the club had decided that every match was vital), Buba looked at us as if he was sizing us up for the first time, and then he came up with some excuse and went and shut himself in the bathroom. Herrera and I watched TV for a while and worked out when we'd go join the card game that Buzatti was organizing in his room. Naturally we weren't expecting Buba to come.

After a little while we heard this wild music coming from the bathroom. I'd already told Herrera about Buba's taste in music and the way he shut himself in his bedroom with that damned cassette player, but he'd never heard it for himself. We sat there listening to the groans and drums for a while, then Herrera, who knew a lot about music and the arts and stuff, said it was by Mango something or other, from Sierra Leone or Liberia, one of the stars of world music anyway, and we left it at that. Then the door opened and Buba came out of the bathroom, sat down beside us, quietly, as if he was interested in the TV show too, and I noticed a slightly odd smell, like the smell of sweat, but it wasn't sweat, a rancid smell, but not exactly rancid either. He smelled of moisture, of mushrooms or toadstools. He smelled strange. It made me nervous, I have to admit, and I know it made Herrera nervous too, both of us were nervous, we both wanted to get out of there, to run to Buzatti's room, where we were sure to find six or seven friends playing cards, stud poker or eleven, a civilized game. But the fact is that neither of us moved, as if Buba's odor and his presence beside us had robbed us of all initiative. It wasn't fear. It had nothing to do with fear. It was something much faster. As if the air surrounding us had condensed and we had turned to liquid. Well, that's what I felt, anyway. And then Buba started talking and told us he needed blood. Herrera's blood and mine.

I think Herrera laughed, not a lot, just a bit. Then one of us switched the TV off, I can't remember who, maybe Herrera, maybe me. And Buba said he could do it, as long as we gave him the drops of blood and kept our mouths shut. What can you do? asked Herrera. Make sure we win the match, I said. I don't know how I knew, but the fact is I had known from the very first moment. Yes, make sure we win the match, said Buba. And then Herrera and I laughed and maybe we looked at each other; Herrera was sitting in an armchair, I was sitting at the foot of my bed, and Buba was sitting at the head of his, waiting deferentially. I think Herrera asked some questions. I asked a question too. Buba replied with numbers. He raised his left hand and showed us his middle, ring and little fingers. He said we had nothing to lose. His thumb and index finger were crossed as if they were forming a lasso or a noose in which a tiny animal was choking. He predicted that Herrera would play. He talked about responsibility to the colors of the shirt and about opportunity. His Spanish was still shaky.

The next thing I remember is that Buba went back into the bathroom and when he came out he was carrying a glass and his straight-edge razor. We're not cutting ourselves with that, said Herrera. The razor is good, said Buba. Not with your razor, said Herrera. Why not? said Buba. Because we don't fucking feel like it, said Herrera. Am I right? He was looking at me. Yes, I said: I'll cut myself with my own razor. I remember that when I got up to go to the bathroom, my legs were shaking. I couldn't find my little razor, I'd probably left it at the apartment, so I grabbed the one provided by the hotel. When I came back in, Herrera was still gone and Buba seemed to be asleep, sitting at the head of his bed, though when I closed the door behind me, he raised his head and looked at me, without saying a word. We said nothing until someone knocked at the door. I went to open it. It was Herrera. The two of us sat down on my bed, Buba sat opposite on his and held the glass between the two beds. Then, with a rapid movement, he lifted one of the fingers on the hand that was holding the glass and made a clean cut in it. Now you, he said to Herrera, who performed the task with a little tiepin, the only sharp thing he'd been able to find. Then it was my turn. When we tried to go to the bathroom to wash our hands, Buba beat us to it. Let me in, Buba, I shouted through the door. All we got by way of reply was the music that Herrera had described a few minutes earlier, somewhat hastily (or that's what I was thinking at least), as world music.

I stayed up late that night. I spent a while in Buzatti's room, then I went to the hotel bar, but there weren't any players left there. I ordered a whiskey and drank it at a table with a good, clear view of the city lights. After a while I sensed that someone was sitting down beside me. I started. It was the trainer, who couldn't sleep either. He asked me what I was doing awake at that hour of the night. I told him I was nervous. But you're not even playing tomorrow, Acevedo, he said. That makes it worse, I said. The trainer looked out at the city, nodding, and rubbed his hands. What are you drinking? he asked. The same as you, I said. Well, he said, it's good for the nerves. Then he started talking about his son and his family, who lived in England, but mostly about his son, and finally we both got up and put our empty glasses on the bar. When I got back to the room, Buba was sleeping quietly in his bed. Normally I wouldn't have switched on the light, but this time I did. Buba didn't even move. I went to the bathroom: all clean and tidy. I put on my pajamas and got into bed and switched off the light. I listened to Buba's regular breathing for a few minutes. I can't remember how long it took me to fall asleep.

The next day we won three-nil. Herrera scored the first goal. That was his first for the season. Buba scored the other two. The journalists made some cautious remarks about a substantial change in our game and highlighted Buba's excellent performance. I watched the match. I know what really happened. Actually, Buba didn't play well. Herrera did, and Delève and Buzatti. The backbone of the team. Actually, for quite a lot of the match, it was like Buba was somewhere else. But he scored two goals and that was enough.

Maybe I should say something about his goals. The first (which was the second goal of the match) came after a corner kick from Palau. In the confusion, Buba swung his leg, connected, and scored. The second one was strange: the other team had already accepted defeat, we were in the 85th minute, all the players were tired, ours especially I think, they were clearly playing it safe, and then someone passed the ball to Buba, expecting him to pass it back, I guess, or just slow the game down, but Buba went running down the sideline, fast, moving much faster than he had all match, and when he got to about four meters from the penalty area, and everyone was expecting him to send it back to the center, he took a shot that surprised the two defenders in front of him and the goalkeeper, a shot with a spin on it like I'd never seen before, the sort of diabolical shot the Brazilians seem to have a monopoly on, which snuck into the top right-hand corner of the goal mouth and sent the crowd wild.

That night, after celebrating the victory, I talked with him. I asked him about the magic, the spell, the blood in the glass. Buba looked at me and went all serious. Bring your ear closer, he said. We were in a disco and we could barely hear one another. He whispered some words that I couldn't understand at first. By that stage I was probably drunk. Then he took his mouth away from my ear and smiled at me. What he had said was: You soon will score better goals. OK, great, I said.

From then on everything went great. We won the next match four-two, even though we were playing away. Herrera scored a goal with a header, Delève put away a penalty kick, and Buba scored the other two, which were completely weird, or that's how they seemed to me, with my inside knowledge; before the trip (I didn't go), I'd taken part in the ceremony of the cut fingers and the glass and the blood.

Three weeks later they summoned me and I made my re-appearance in the second half, in the 75th minute. We were playing the top-ranked team on their home ground and we won one-nil. I scored the goal in the 88th minute. I took the pass from Buba or that's what everyone thought, but I have my doubts. All I know is that Buba took off down the right-hand side of the field, and I started running down the left-hand side. There were four defenders, one chasing Buba, two in the middle, and one about three yards away from me. I still can't explain what happened next. The defenders in the middle seemed to freeze on the spot. I kept running with the right wingback on my heels. Buba came up to the penalty area with the left wingback close behind him too. Then he dummied and centered. I went into the penalty area with no hope of receiving the pass, but what with the center backs in a daze or dizzy all of a sudden and the weird swing of the ball, the fact is I found myself miraculously in possession inside the area, with their goalkeeper coming forward and the right wingback coming up behind my left shoulder, not knowing whether to foul me or not, so I just took a shot and scored and we won.

I had a safe place on the team for the following Sunday. And from then on I began to score more goals than I'd ever scored in my life. Herrera was on a roll as well. Everyone loved Buba. And they loved Herrera and me too. From one day to the next we became the kings of the city. It was all working out for us. The club began an unstoppable climb. We were winning matches and hearts.

And our blood ritual was repeated without fail before every match. In fact, after the first time, Herrera and I bought ourselves straight-edge razors like Buba's; every time we played away, the first thing we put in our bags was the straight-edge, and when we played at home, we got together the night before at our apartment (they'd stopped keeping us together in a hotel) and performed the ceremony: Buba collected his blood and ours in a glass and then shut himself in the bathroom, and while we heard the music coming out of there, Herrera would talk about books he'd read or plays he'd seen and I just listened and agreed with everything he said, until Buba reappeared and we looked at him as if to ask if everything was all right, and Buba would smile at us and go to the kitchen to fetch a sponge and a bucket before returning to the bathroom, where he'd spend at least fifteen minutes cleaning and tidying up, and when we went into the bathroom, everything was exactly the same as before. Sometimes, when I went to a disco with Herrera and Buba stayed home (because he didn't like discos much) Herrera and I would get talking and he'd ask me what I thought Buba did with our blood in the bathroom, because you couldn't tell—when Buba was finished there wasn't a trace of blood anywhere, the glass we used was sparkling, the floor was spotless, it was like the cleaning lady had just left—and I said to Herrera I didn't know, I had no idea what Buba did when he shut himself in there, and Herrera looked at me and said: If I was living with him I'd be scared, and I looked at Herrera thinking: Are you serious? but Herrera said, I'm just kidding, Buba's our friend; it's thanks to him I'm on the team and the club is going to win the championship; it's thanks to him we're tasting sweet success, and that was the truth.

Besides, I was never scared of Buba. Sometimes, when we were watching TV in our apartment before going to bed, I'd glance at him out of the corner of my eye and think how strange it all was. But I didn't think about it for long. Soccer is strange.

In the end, after starting the year so disastrously, we won the League Championship and paraded through the center of Barcelona in the midst of a jubilant crowd and spoke from the town hall balcony to another jubilant crowd, which chanted our names, and we dedicated our victory to the Virgin of Montserrat, in the monastery of Montserrat, a virgin as black as Buba, strange as it may seem, and we gave interviews until we were hoarse. I spent my vacation in Chile. Buba went to Africa. Herrera and his girlfriend took off to the Caribbean.

We met up again at preseason training, in a sports center in the east of Holland, near an ugly, gray city that made me feel extremely apprehensive.

Everyone was there, except for Buba. He'd had some kind of problem back in his country. Herrera seemed exhausted, though he was sporting a celebrity tan. He told me he'd considered getting married. I told him about my vacation in Chile, but as you know, when it's summer in Europe, it's winter in Chile, so my vacation hadn't been especially exciting. The family was well. That was about it. We were worried about Buba and the holdup. We didn't want to admit it, but we were worried. Herrera and I were soon convinced that without him we were lost. Our trainer, on the other hand, tried to play down Buba's lack of punctuality.

One morning Buba arrived on a flight that had come via

Rome and Frankfurt and took his place on the team again. The preseason matches, however, were disastrous. We were beaten by a team from the Dutch third division. We tied with a team of amateurs from the city where we were staying. Neither Herrera nor I dared to ask Buba to do the blood ritual, although we had our razors ready. In fact, and it took me a while to realize this, it was like we were afraid to ask Buba for a bit of his magic. Of course we went on being friends, and one night the three of us went out to a Dutch disco, but instead of talking about blood, we talked about the rumors that always circulate before the season starts, the players who were changing teams, the new signings, the Champion's League, in which we'd be playing that year, the contracts that were expiring or had to be renegotiated. We also talked about movies and the vacation that had just come to an end, and Herrera talked about books, but he was on his own there, mainly because he was the only one of us who read.

Then we went back to Barcelona, and Buba and I went back to our routine, just the two of us in that apartment opposite the training ground, and the Champion's League began, and the night before the first match, Herrera turned up at our place and bit the bullet. He asked Buba what was happening. Isn't there going to be any magic this year? And Buba smiled and said it wasn't magic. And Herrera said, What the fuck is it then? And Buba shrugged his shoulders and said it was something only he understood. And then he made a face like he was saying, It's no big deal. And Herrera said he wanted to keep on going, he believed in Buba, whatever it was he'd been doing. And Buba said he was tired, and when he said that I looked at his face: he didn't look nineteen or twenty at all, he looked at least ten years older, like a player who had worn his body out. And, to my surprise, Herrera accepted what Buba had said, calmly, just like that. He said, OK, let's drop it. What about dinner? My treat. That's the way he was, Herrera. A great guy.

So we went out to dinner at one of the best restaurants in the city, and a press photographer who was there took a picture of us, the one I've got hanging in the dining room: Herrera, Buba and me, dressed up and smiling, with a lavish meal (if you'll pardon the cliché) spread out in front of us (it really was lavish); we look like we're ready to take on the world, although deep down we weren't at all sure (especially Herrera and me) that we could take on anyone at all. And nothing was said about magic or blood while we were there: we talked about movies and travel (for pleasure not work), and that was about all. When we left the restaurant, after having signed autographs for the waiters and the cook and the kitchen hands, we went walking through the empty streets of the city, such a beautiful city, the city of sanity and common sense, as some devotees call it, but also the city of splendor, where you could feel at ease with yourself, and for me, looking back, it's the city of my youth—anyway, as I was saying, we went walking through the streets of Barcelona, because, as every athlete knows, the best thing to do after a heavy meal is stretch your legs, and when we'd been walking around for a while, looking at the floodlit buildings (Herrera named the great architects who'd designed them like they were people he'd met), Buba said with a rather sad smile that, if we wanted to, we could repeat last year's experiment.

That was the word he used. Experiment. Herrera and I kept quiet. Then we went back to my car and drove to the apartment without saying a single word. I cut myself with my razor. Herrera used a knife from the kitchen. When Buba came out of the bathroom, he looked at us, and, for the first time he didn't shut the door behind him when he went to get the sponge and a bucket of water from the kitchen. I remember Herrera stood up but then sat down again straightaway. Then Buba shut himself in the bathroom and when he came out it was all like before. I suggested we celebrate with one last whiskey. Herrera accepted. Buba shook his head. I guess none of us felt like talking; the only one who spoke was Buba. He said: This isn't necessary, we're already rich. That was all. Then Herrera and I downed our whiskeys and we all went to bed. The next day we started off in the League with a six-zero victory. Buba scored three goals, Herrera scored one and I scored two. It was a glorious season, people still remember it, which is amazing, considering how long ago it was, although if I really think about it, if I exercise my memory, it seems right and proper (though I say so myself) that my second and final season playing with Buba in Europe should have been saved from oblivion. You saw the matches on TV. If you'd been in Barcelona you'd have gone crazy. We won the national League by more than fifteen points and were European Champions without having lost a single match, just two draws: with Milan at San Siro and with Bayern on their home ground. Every other game we won.

Buba became the man of the moment, top goal scorer in the Spanish League and the Champion's League, and his value soared. Halfway through the season, his agent tried to renegotiate the contract and more than triple the annual payment, and the club had no choice but to sell him to Juventus at the beginning of the following preseason. There were lots of clubs vying for Herrera too, but since he'd come up through the ranks and been virtually raised in the junior teams, he didn't want to leave, though I know for sure he had offers from Manchester, where he would have got more money. I had a string of offers too, but after letting Buba go, the club couldn't afford to lose me, so they upped my fee and I stayed.

By then I'd met a Catalan woman who would soon become my wife and I think that influenced my decision not to leave. I don't regret it. That season we were champions in the Spanish League again, but in the Champion's League we came up against Buba's team in the semifinals and we were eliminated. They beat us three-zero in Italy and Buba scored one of the goals, one of the most beautiful goals I've ever seen, from a foul, or a free kick, as you guys say, more than twenty yards from the goal, what the Brazilians would call a dead leaf, an autumn leaf, when the ball looks like it's heading over the top and then suddenly it drops like a falling leaf, Didí could pull it off, so they say, but I'd never seen Buba do it, and after that goal I remember Herrera looked at me—I was in the wall and Herrera was behind me, marking an Italian player— and when our goalkeeper went to get the ball from the net, Herrera looked at me and smiled as if to say, Well, what do you know, and I smiled too. It was the first goal for the Italians and after that Buba virtually disappeared from the game. They took him off in the fiftieth minute. Before leaving the field he hugged Herrera and me. After the match we spent some time with him in the passage to the locker rooms.

In the return match on our home ground we tied with the Italians zero-zero. It was one of the strangest games I've ever played. Everything seemed to be happening in slow motion and in the end the Italians eliminated us. But overall it was a memorable season. We won the Spanish League again, Herrera and I were both selected for our national teams for the World Cup, and Buba went from strength to strength. His team won the Italian League (the famous *Scudetto*) and the Champion's League. He was *the* star player. Sometimes we'd call him and chat for a while. Not long before we left for summer vacation (it was going to be shorter than usual because that year the international players had to start preparing for the World Cup almost right away) the news hit the front page of the sports papers: Buba had been killed in a car accident on the way to the Turin airport.

We were stunned. What more can I say? Honestly, we were just stunned. The World Cup was terrible. Chile was eliminated in the quarterfinals, without having won a single match. Spain didn't even get to the quarterfinals, although they did win once. My performance was appalling as I'm sure you remember. The less said the better. Buba's team? No, they were eliminated in the qualifying round by Cameroon or Nigeria, I can't remember which. Even if he'd been alive, Buba wouldn't have been able to go to the World Cup. As a player I mean.

The seasons went by and there were other championships and World Cups and other friends. I was in Barcelona for another six years. And four more years in Spain after that. Throughout that time, I had other days and nights of glory, of course, but it was never the same. I finished my soccer career with Colo-Colo, playing as a midfielder, not a left winger (left wingers have an expiration date). Then I set up my sports store. I could have been a trainer, I did the course, but by then I was tired of it, to tell you the truth. Herrera played for a couple more years. Then he retired at the height of his fame. He played more than a hundred international matches (I only played forty) and when he quit, the Barcelona fans paid him a really exceptional tribute. Now he has I don't know how many businesses there, and he's doing well, as you'd expect.

We didn't see each other for many years. Until recently, when they made a TV program, a nostalgic kind of show, about the team who won the first Champion's League. I got the invitation, and although I don't like traveling any more, I accepted, because it was an opportunity to meet up with old friends. What can I say? The city's just as beautiful as ever. They put us up in a first-class hotel and my wife went straight off to see her family and friends. I decided to lie down on the bed and take a nap, but after a quarter of an hour I realized I wouldn't be able to sleep. Then a kid from the production company came to get me and took me to the TV studios. I ran into Pepito Vila in the makeup room. He was completely bald and I almost didn't recognize him. Then Delève turned up and that was the killer. They were all so old. But my spirits rose a bit when I saw Herrera, before going onto the set. Him I would have recognized anywhere. We hugged and exchanged a few words, enough to make it clear that we'd be having dinner together that night, whatever else happened.

The program was long and detailed. There was stuff about the Cup, what it had meant for the club, about Buba and his first year in Europe, but there was also stuff about Buzatti and Delève, Palau and Pepito Vila, and me, and especially about Herrera and his long sports career, an example for the young. There were six ex-players, three journalists and two celebrity fans: a movie actor and a Brazilian singer who turned out to be the most fanatical supporter I've ever come across. She was called Liza Do Elisa, though I don't think that was her real name, and when the interviews were finished (I said hardly

anything, a few dumb remarks, my stomach was all in knots)
she came to dinner with us, with Herrera and me and Pepito
Vila and one of the journalists, maybe she was a friend of
journalist's, I don't know, anyhow, suddenly I found myself
in a dimly lit restaurant with all these people, and then in
a disco, which was even darker, except for the dance floor,
where I danced, sometimes on my own, sometimes with Liza
Do Elisa, and then, some time after midnight, I ended up in
a bar near the port, sitting at a grimy table, drinking coffee
with a shot, along with Herrera and the Brazilian singer—the
others had gone.

I don't remember which of them brought it up. Maybe
Liza Do Elisa was talking about magic, she could've been, or
maybe it was Herrera who got her onto it, I think she mentioned black magic and white magic, and then she started
telling stories, true stories, things that had happened to her
as a child, or when she was young and making her way in
the world of show business. I remember looking at her and
thinking she was a formidable woman: she was speaking in
the same forceful, vehement way as she'd spoken in front of
the TV cameras. She'd had to struggle to make it and she
was permanently on guard, as if she could be attacked at any
moment. She was a pretty woman, about thirty-five, with a
nice rack. You could tell her life hadn't been easy. But Herrera
wasn't interested in her life story, I realized that straightaway.
Herrera wanted to talk about magic, voodoo, Candomblé
rituals, black people's business, in short. And Liza Do Elisa
was happy to oblige.

So I finished my coffee and let them talk, and since, to be
honest, I wasn't all that interested in the topic of their conversation, I ordered a whiskey and then another, and when

daylight was already beginning to shine in through the windows of the bar, Herrera said he had a story a bit like the ones Liza Do Elisa had been telling, and he was going to tell it and see what she thought. Then I shut my eyes, like I was sleepy, although I wasn't sleepy at all, and listened to Herrera telling Buba's story, our story, but without saying that Buba was Buba and pretending that he and I were some French players he'd met a while back, and Liza Do Elisa went quiet (I think it was the first time she'd been quiet all night) until Herrera came to the end, to Buba's death, and only then did she speak up and say yes, it was possible, and Herrera asked about the blood that the three players spilled into the glass, and Liza Do Elisa said it was part of the ceremony, and Herrera asked about the music that came from the bathroom when the black guy shut himself in there, and Liza Do Elisa said it was part of the ceremony, and then Herrera asked about what happened to the blood when the black guy took it into the bathroom, and about the sponge and the bucket of water with bleach, and he also wanted to know what Liza Do Elisa thought the guy did in the bathroom, and the Brazilian singer replied to all his questions by saying that it was part of the ceremony, until Herrera started getting annoyed and said obviously it was part of the ceremony but he wanted to know what the ceremony was. And then Liza Do Elisa said, Nobody raises his voice to me, especially not—and I quote—if he wants to fuck me, to which Herrera replied with a laugh that reminded me of the good old days—the Herrera of the Champion's League and the two Spanish Leagues we won together, I mean, the two we won with Buba and the five we won overall—and then he said he hadn't meant to offend her (Liza Do Elisa took offense at the slightest little thing), and repeated his question.

The singer seemed to be deep in thought for a while, then she looked at Herrera and me (but she looked much more intensely at Herrera) and said she didn't know for sure. Maybe he drank the blood, maybe he poured it down the toilet, maybe he pissed or shat on it, maybe he didn't do any of those things, maybe he took his clothes off and smeared himself with blood and then took a shower, but it was all speculation. Then the three of us sat there in silence until Liza Do Elisa said that whatever he did, one thing was for sure: the guy had suffered and loved deeply.

And then Herrera asked her what she thought about this black guy who had played in the French team: did his magic work? No, said Liza Do Elisa. He was crazy. How could it work? And Herrera asked, How come his teammates started playing better? Because they were good players, said the singer. And then I weighed in and asked what she meant when she said he'd suffered deeply, how do you mean? And she replied, With his whole body, but more than that, with his whole mind.

"What do you mean, Liza?" I insisted.

"That he was crazy," said the singer.

The bar's metal gates had been pulled down. On a wall I noticed various photos of our team. The singer asked us (not just Herrera, me too) if we'd been talking about Buba. Not one muscle in Herrera's face moved. I might have nodded. Liza Do Elisa crossed herself. I got up and went to take a look at the photos. There we were, the eleven of us: Herrera standing with his arms crossed next to Miquel Serra, the goalkeeper, and Palau, and, in front of them, squatting down, Buba and me. I was smiling, as if I didn't have a care in the world, and Buba was serious, looking straight at the camera.

I went to the bathroom and when I came back Herrera was paying at the bar, and the singer was standing beside the table, smoothing her close-fitting, deep red dress. Before we left, the bartender, or maybe he was the owner, the guy who'd put up with us until dawn, anyway, asked me to sign another one of the photos decorating the wall. It was a photo of me on my own, taken just after I arrived in the city. I asked him his name. He said he was called Narcis. To Narcis, I signed it, affectionately.

It was already getting light when we left. We walked through the streets of Barcelona, like in the old days. I wasn't surprised to notice that Herrera had his arm around the singer's waist. Then we hailed a taxi and they accompanied me back to my hotel.

PHOTOS

When it comes to poets, give me the French, thinks Arturo Belano, lost in Africa, leafing through a sort of photo album in which Francophone poetry celebrates itself, sons of bitches, he thinks, sitting on the ground, a ground of red clay, or something like that, but it's not clay, not even clayey, though it is red, or rather coppery in color, or reddish, except at midday when it's yellow, the book lying between his legs, a fat book, nine hundred and thirty pages, so close enough to a thousand pages long, a hardback, *La poésie contemporaine de langue française depuis 1945*, edited by Serge Brindeau, published by Bordas, a compendium of little texts about all the poets writing in French around the world, be it in France or Belgium, Canada or North Africa, sub-Saharan Africa or the Middle East, so it's not such a miracle to find the book here, thinks Belano, because if it includes African poets, some copies would have come to Africa, obviously, in the luggage of the poets themselves or the luggage of some tragically naïve bookseller committed to the Francophone cause, though it's still a miracle that one of those copies should happen to turn up just here, in this village, forsaken by god and abandoned by the human race, where there's no one left but me and the ghosts of the contributors and not much else except the book and the changing colors of the earth, it's weird, but the earth does actually change color every so often, dark yellow in the morning, yellow at midday, with watery streaks, like crystallized, dirty water, and who'd want to look at it after that, thinks Belano, looking up at the sky through which three clouds are floating, like three signs in a blue field, the field of conjectures or the field of mystical doctrines, amazed by the elegance of the clouds and their unspeakably slow procession, then looking at the photos, his nose almost touching the page, examining those faces with all their contortions, which isn't the word exactly, yes it is, Jean Pérol, for example, who looks like he's listening to a joke, or Gérald Neveu (whom Belano has read), who looks like he's dazzled by the sun or living in a month that's a monstrous coupling of July and August, something that only Africans can stand or the poets of Germany and France, or Vera Feyder, who is holding and stroking a cat, as if holding and stroking were one and the same, and they are, thinks Belano, or Jean-Philippe Salabreuil (whom he has read), so young, so handsome, he looks like a movie star, looking at me from the far side of death with a half smile, telling me or the African reader to whom this book belonged that it's all right, that the constant motion of the spirit is futile and it's all right, and Belano shuts his eyes without lowering his head, then he opens them again and turns the page and here we have Patrice Cauda, who looks like he hits his wife—what am I saying, his wife, I mean his girlfriend—and Jean Dubacq, who looks like he works in a bank, like a sad bank clerk with little hope left, a Catholic, and Jacques Arnold, who looks like the manager of the bank that employs the unfortunate Dubacq, and Janine Mitaud, large mouth, sparkling eyes, a middle-aged woman with short hair, a slim neck and, to judge from her expression, a subtle sense of humor, and Philippe Jaccottet (whom he has read), who's thin and has a kind-looking face, though maybe, thinks Belano, it's one of those kind-looking faces you should never trust, and Claude de Burine, the incarnation of Little Orphan Annie—even her dress, or what the photo shows of her dress, is identical to Little Orphan Annie's—but who is this Claude de Burine, Belano asks himself aloud, alone in an African village whose inhabitants have all fled or been killed, sitting on the ground with his knees up, while his fingers flick with a singular rapidity through the pages of *La poésie contemporaine* in search of information about this poet, which he eventually finds: Claude de Burine, he reads, was born in Saint-Léger-des-Vignes (Nièvre), in 1931, and she is the author of *Lettres à l'enfance* (Rougerie, 1957), *La Gardienne* (Le soleil dans la tête—good name for a publishing house—1960), *L'allumeur de réverbères* (Rougerie, 1963) and *Hanches* (Librairie Saint-Germain-des-Près, 1969), and that's all the biographical information there is, as if at the age of thirty-eight, after the publication of *Hanches*, Little Orphan Annie had disappeared, although the author of the introductory note says: *Claude de Burine, avant toute autre chose, dit l'amour, l'amour inépuisable*, and when Belano reads that, it all makes sense in his overheated brain: someone who *dit l'amour* could perfectly well disappear at the age of thirty-eight, especially, *especially* if that person is the double of Little Orphan Annie, with the same round eyes, the same hair, the eyebrows of someone who has seen the inside of a foundling hospital, an expression of perplexity and pain, a pain alleviated to some degree by caricature, but it's pain all the same, and then Belano says to himself, I'm going to find a lot of pain here, and turns back to the photos and discovers, under the photo of Claude de Burine, between the photo of Philippe Jaccottet and the photo of Jacques Réda, Marc Alyn and Dominique Tron sharing the same snapshot, a lighter moment, Dominique Tron who's so different from Claude de Burine, on the one hand, the existentialist, the beatnik, the rocker, and on the other, meekness incarnate, a woman forsaken and banished, thinks Belano, as if Dominique lived in a whirlwind while the all-suffering Claude looked on from a metaphysical distance, and again Belano's curiosity is piqued and he consults the index and then after reading *né à Bin el Oidane (Maroc) le 11 décembre 1950*, he realizes that Dominique Tron is a man, and he thinks as he brushes a (completely imaginary) mosquito away from his ear, I must be suffering from sunstroke, and reads Tron's list of publications: *Stéréophonies* (Seghers, 1965, that is, at the age of fifteen), *Kamikaze Galapagos* (Seghers, 1967, that is, at the age of seventeen), *La Souffrance est inutile* (Seghers, 1968, that is, at the age of eighteen), *D'Épuisement en épuisement jusqu'à l'aurore, Elisabeth*, an autobiographical oratorio, followed by a mystery, *Boucles de feu* (Seghers, 1968, that is, again, at the age of eighteen), and *De la Science-fiction c'est nous à l'interprétation des corps* (Eric Losfeld, 1972, that is, at the age of twenty-two), and that's all there is, largely because *La poésie contemporaine* was published in 1973, had it been published in 1974 there surely would have been more titles, and then Belano thinks about his own youth, when he used to churn it out like Tron, and was perhaps even better looking than Tron, he thinks, squinting at the photo, but to publish a poem, in Mexico, all those years ago when he lived in Mexico City, he'd had to sweat blood, because Mexico is Mexico, he reflects, and France is France, and then he shuts his eyes and sees a torrent of ghostly, emblematic Mexicans flowing like a gray breath of air along a dry river bed, and before opening his eyes, holding the book firmly in both hands, he sees Claude de Burine again, the photo-portrait of Claude de Burine, in her lonely poet's tower, watching the adolescent cyclone that is Dominique Tron, who wrote *La souffrance est inutile*, and perhaps he wrote it for her, for Claude, a book that is a burning bridge, which Dominique himself will not cross, but Claude will, oblivious to the bridge, oblivious to everything, she will cross it and be burnt in the attempt, thinks Belano, as all poets are burnt, even the bad ones, on those burning bridges that are so enticing, so fascinating when you're eighteen, or twenty-one, but then so dull, so monotonous, beginning and ending so predictably, those bridges that he crossed like Ulysses on his way home, bridges theorized and conjured up before his eyes like fantastic Ouija boards, enormous burning structures repeated over and over into the depths of the screen, which may stop poets at eighteen or twenty-one, but twenty-three-year-old poets can cross them with their eyes closed, like sleepwalking warriors, thinks Belano as he imagines the helpless, the fragile, the terribly fragile Claude de Burine running toward the arms of Dominique Tron, on a course he chooses to imagine as erratic, although there is something in Claude's eyes, and in Dominique's, and in the eyes of the burning bridge, that strikes him as familiar, something that—like the changing colors all around the empty village—speaks in a down-to-earth way of the arid, sad and terrible end to come, and then Belano shuts his eyes and keeps still, and opens his eyes again and turns to another page, although this time he's determined to look at the photos and nothing else, and that's how he finds Pierre Morency, a good-looking kid, Jean-Guy Pilon, a difficult character, not photogenic, Fernand Ouellette, a man who's going bald (and remembering that the book was published in 1973, all things considered, it's pretty safe to assume that he's completely bald by now), and Nicole Brossard, a girl with straight hair, with a part in the middle, big eyes, a square jaw, pretty, Belano finds her pretty, but he doesn't want to know how old Nicole is or what books she has written so he turns the page, and suddenly enters (though in the village where he happens to be stranded there is no such thing as a sudden entry) the kingdom of the thousand and one nights of literature and memory, because he has come to the photos of Mohammed Khaïr-Eddine and Kateb Yacine and Anna Greki and Malek Haddad and Abdellatif Laabi and Ridha Zili, Arab poets who write in French, and he remembers having seen some of those poets already, many years ago, maybe in 1972, before the publication of the book he is holding, or in 1971, or perhaps he's mistaken and is seeing them for the first time, with a persistent and as yet unexplained feeling, somewhere between perplexity—a singularly sweet perplexity—and envy, wishing he had belonged to that group, it was 1973 or '74, he remembers now, in a book on Arab poets or North African poets that a Uruguayan woman carried around with her for a couple of days everywhere she went in Mexico City, a book with an ochre or yellow cover, the color of desert sands, and then Belano turns the page and more photos appear, Kamal Ibrahim (whom he has read), Salah Stétié, Marwan Hoss, Fouad Gabriel Naffah (a diabolically ugly poet), and Nadia Tuéni, Andrée Chédid and Vénus Khoury, and Belano cranes forward, his face almost touching the page, to see the women poets in more detail, and Nadia and Vénus seem truly beautiful, with Nadia he'd fuck until dawn, he thinks (assuming that night will fall again sometime, since where he is, the evenings drag on as if the village were following the sun in its westward march, Belano thinks, with a certain disquiet) and with Vénus he'd fuck until three in the morning, and then I'd get up, light a cigarette and go out for a walk along the esplanade in Malgrat de Mar, but with Nadia he'd go on till dawn, and the things he'd do with Vénus he'd do with Nadia too, but he'd do things with Nadia that he wouldn't do with anyone else, thinks Belano as he stares without blinking at Nadia's smile, his nose almost touching the page, and Nadia's lively eyes, her dark shining abundant hair, a protective cowl of shadow, and then Belano looks up and can no longer see the three solitary clouds in the African sky over the village where he has washed up, a village the sun is dragging westward—the clouds have disappeared, as if they were superfluous now that he has seen the smile of the Arab poet of the thousand and one nights, and then Belano breaks his promise, looks up the name Tuéni in the index and turns intrepidly to the pages in the critical section where he knows he will find her biographical note, a note that says that Nadia was born in Beirut in 1935, which means that when the book was published she was thirty-eight, although the photo is earlier, and the note also says that she has published a number of books, including *Les Textes blonds* (Beyrouth, Éd. An-Nahar, 1963), *L'Age d'écume* (Seghers, 1966), *Juin et les mécréantes* (Seghers, 1968), and *Poèmes pour une histoire* (Seghers, 1972), and in the paragraphs about her, Belano reads *habituée aux chimères*, and he reads *chez ce poète des marées, des ouragans, des naufrages,* and he reads *fille elle-même d'un père druze et d'une mère française,* and he reads *mariée à un Chrétien orthodoxe,* and he reads *Nadia Tuéni (née Nadia Mohammed Ali Hamadé),* and he reads *Timidir la Chrétienne, Sabba la Musulmane, Dâhoun la Juive, Sioun la Druze,* and he stops reading and looks up because he thinks he heard something, the cry of a vulture or a turkey buzzard, even though he knows there are no turkey buzzards here, but that can be fixed, given time, not necessarily years of time, hours or even minutes would do, at some point you stop knowing what you used to know, it's as simple and as hard as that, even a Mexican turkey buzzard could turn up in this lousy village, thinks Belano with tears in his eyes, and it's not the sound of the turkey buzzards making him cry but the physical presence of Nadia Tuéni's image looking at him from a page in the book with a petrified smile that seems to open out like blown glass in the landscape surrounding Belano, which is also made of glass, and then he thinks he hears words, the words he has just read but cannot read now because he is crying, *l'air torride, habituée aux chimères,* and a story about Druses, Jews, Muslims and Christians, from which Nadia emerges at the age of thirty-eight (the same age as Claude de Burine) with the hair of an Arab princess, immaculate, perfectly serene, like the accidental muse of certain poets, or their provisional muse, the one who says, Don't worry, or who says, Worry, but not too much, the one who doesn't speak in dry and definite words but whispers, whose parting gift is a kind look, and then Belano thinks of the age the real Nadia Tuéni must be, in 1996, and he realizes that now she is sixty-one, and he stops crying, *l'air torride* has dried his tears once again, and he starts turning the pages, he returns to the mug shots of the Francophone poets with an obstinacy worthy of a higher enterprise, like a scavenging bird he returns to the face of Tchicaya U Tam'si, born in Mpili in 1931, the face of Matala Mukadi, born in Luiska in 1942, the face of Samuel-Martin Eno Belinga, born in Ebolowa in 1935, the face of Elologué Epanya Yondo, born in Douala in 1930, and so many other faces, faces of poets who write in French, photogenic or not, the face of Michel Van Schendel, born in Asnières in 1929, the face of Raoul Duguay (whom he has read), born in Val d'Or in 1939, the face of Suzanne Paradis, born in Beaumont in 1936, the face of Daniel Biga (whom he has read), born in Saint-Sylvestre in 1940, the face of Denise Jallais, born in Saint-Nazaire in 1932 and almost as pretty as Nadia, Belano thinks with a kind of comprehensive tremor, while evening keeps dragging the village westward, and turkey buzzards start to appear in the tops of some small trees, except that Denise is blonde and Nadia is dark, both very beautiful, sixty-one and sixty-four respectively, I hope they're alive, he thinks, his gaze fixed not on the photos in the book but on the line of the treetops against the sky where the birds are teetering, crows or vultures or turkey buzzards, and then Belano remembers a poem by Gregory Corso, in which the hapless North American poet spoke of his one true love, an Egyptian woman dead two thousand five hundred years ago, and Belano remembers Corso's street-kid face and a figure from Egyptian art that he saw a long time ago on a matchbox, a girl getting out of a bath or a river or a swimming pool, and the beat poet (the enthusiastic, hapless Corso) is watching her from the other side of time, and the Egyptian girl with long legs senses that she is being watched, and that's all, her flirting with Corso is as brief as a sigh in the immensity of time, but time itself and its remote sovereignty can also pass like a sigh, thinks Belano as he watches the birds up in the branches, silhouettes on the horizon, an electrocardiogram agitated by the ruffling or spreading of wings as it waits for death, my death, thinks Belano, and then he shuts his eyes for a long time, as if he were thinking or crying with his eyes shut, and when he opens them again the crows are there, the electroencephalogram trembling on the African horizon, and then Belano shuts the book and stands up, still holding it, grateful, and begins to walk westward, toward the coast, with the book of Francophone poets under his arm, grateful, and his thought speeds ahead of his steps through the jungles and deserts of Liberia, as it did when he was an adolescent in Mexico, and soon his steps lead him away from the village.

MEETING WITH ENRIQUE LIHN

for Celina Manzoni

In 1999, after returning from Venezuela, I dreamed that I was being taken to Enrique Lihn's apartment, in a country that could well have been Chile, in a city that could well have been Santiago, bearing in mind that Chile and Santiago once resembled Hell, a resemblance that, in some subterranean layer of the real city and the imaginary city, will forever remain. Of course I knew that Lihn was dead, but when they offered to take me to meet him I accepted without hesitation. Maybe I thought that the people I was with were playing a joke, or that a miracle might be possible. But probably I just wasn't thinking, or had misunderstood the invitation. In any case we came to a seven-story building, with a façade painted a faded yellow and a bar on the ground floor, a bar of considerable dimensions, with a long counter and several booths, and my friends (although it seems odd to describe them like that; let's just say the enthusiasts who had offered to take me to meet the poet) led me to a booth, and there was Lihn. At first I could hardly recognize him, it wasn't the face I had seen on his books; he'd grown thinner and younger, he'd become more handsome, and his eyes looked much brighter than the black-and-white eyes in the back-cover photographs. In fact,

Lihn didn't look like Lihn at all, he looked like a Hollywood actor, a B-list actor, the kind who stars in TV movies or films that are never shown in European cinemas and go straight to video. But at the same time he was Lihn, although he no longer looked like him; I was in no doubt about that. The enthusiasts greeted him, calling him Enrique with a fake-sounding familiarity and asked him questions I couldn't understand, and then they introduced us, although to tell the truth I didn't need to be introduced, because for a time, a short time, I had corresponded with him, and his letters had, in a way, kept me going; I'm talking about 1981 or 1982, when I was living like a recluse in a house outside Gerona with practically no money and no prospects of ever getting any, and literature was a vast minefield occupied by enemies, except for a few classic authors (just a few), and every day I had to walk through that minefield, with only the poems of Archilocus to guide me, and any false move could have been fatal. It's like that for all young writers. There comes a time when you have no support, not even from friends, forget about mentors, and there's no one to give you a hand; publication, prizes and grants are reserved for the others, the ones who said "Yes, sir," over and over, or those who praised the literary mandarins, a never-ending horde distinguished only by their aptitude for discipline and punishment—nothing escapes them and they forgive nothing. Anyway, as I was saying, all young writers feel like that at some point or other in their lives. But at the time I was twenty-eight years old and in no sense could I consider myself a young writer. I was adrift. I wasn't the typical Latin American writer living in Europe thanks to some government sinecure. I was a nobody and not inclined to show any mercy or beg for it. Then I started corresponding with Enrique Lihn. Naturally I was the one who initiated the correspondence. I didn't have to wait long for his reply. A long, crotchety letter, as we might say in Chile: gloomy and irritable. In my reply I told him about my life, my house in the country, on one of the hills outside Gerona, the medieval city before it, the countryside or the void behind. I also told him about my dog, Laika, and said that in my opinion Chilean literature, with one or two exceptions, was shit. It was evident from his next letter that we were already friends. What followed was what typically happens when a famous poet befriends an unknown. He read my poems and included some of them in a kind of reading he organized to present the work of the younger generation at the Chilean-North American Institute of Culture. In his letter he identified a set of hopefuls destined, so he thought, to be the six tigers of Chilean poetry in the year 2000. The six tigers were Bertoni, Maquieira, Gonzalo Muñoz, Martínez, Rodrigo Lira and myself. I think. Maybe there were seven tigers. But I think there were only six. And it would have been hard for the six of us to be anything much in 2000, because by then Rodrigo Lira, the best of the lot, had killed himself and what was left of him had been rotting for years in some cemetery, or else was ash, blowing around the streets mingled with the filth of Santiago. Cats would have been more appropriate than tigers. Bertoni, as far as I know, is a kind of hippie who lives by the sea, collecting shells and seaweed. Maquieira made a careful study of Cardenal and Coronel Urtecho's anthology of North American poetry, published two books and then settled down to drinking. Gonzalo Muñoz went to Mexico, so I heard, where he disappeared, not into ethylic oblivion like Lowry's consul, but into the advertising industry. Martínez made a careful study of *Duchamp du signe* and then died.

As for Rodrigo Lira, well, I already explained what became of him. Not so much tigers as cats, whichever way you look at it. The kittens of a far-flung province. Anyway, what I wanted to say is that I knew Lihn, so no introduction was necessary. Nevertheless the enthusiasts proceeded to introduce me and neither I nor Lihn objected. So there we were, in a booth, and voices were saying, This is Roberto Bolaño, and I held out my hand, my arm was enveloped by the darkness of the booth, and I grasped Lihn's hand, a slightly cold hand, which squeezed mine for a few seconds—the hand of a sad person, I thought, a hand and a handshake that corresponded perfectly to the face that was scrutinizing me without showing any sign of recognition. The correspondence was gestural, bodily, and opened onto an opaque eloquence that had nothing to say, or at least not to me. Once that moment was past, the enthusiasts started talking again and the silence receded; they were all asking Lihn for his opinions on the most disparate issues and events, and at that point my disdain evaporated at once, be-cause I realized that they were just like I had once been: young poets with no support, kids who'd been shut out by the new center-left Chilean government and didn't have any backing or patronage, all they had was Lihn, a Lihn who looked much more handsome and prepossessing than the real Enrique Lihn as he appeared in the author photos, a Lihn who resembled his poems, who had adopted their age, who lived in a building similar to his poems, and who could disappear, as his poems sometimes did, with a characteristic elegance and poise. When I realized this, I remember I felt better. I mean I began to make sense of the situation and find it amusing. I had nothing to fear: I was at home, with friends, with a writer I had always admired. It wasn't a horror movie. Or not an out-and-out horror movie, but a horror movie leavened with large doses of black humor. And just as I thought of black humor, Lihn extracted a little bottle of pills from his pocket. I have to take one every three hours, he said. The enthusiasts fell silent once again. A waiter brought a glass of water. The pill was big. That's what I thought when I saw it fall into the glass of water. But in fact it wasn't big. It was dense. Lihn began to break it up with a spoon and I realized that the pill looked like an onion with countless layers. I leaned forward and peered into the glass. For a moment I was quite sure that it was an infinite pill. The curved glass had a magnifying effect, like a lens: inside, the pale pink pill was disintegrating as if giving birth to a galaxy or the universe. But galaxies are born or die (I forget which) suddenly, and what I could see through the curved side of that glass was unfolding in slow motion, each incomprehensible stage drawn out as I watched, every retraction and shudder. Then, feeling exhausted, I sat back, and my gaze, detached from the medicinal solution, rose to meet Lihn's eyes, which seemed to be saying: No comment, it's bad enough having to swallow this concoction every three hours, don't go looking for symbolic meanings—the water, the onion, the slow march of the stars. The enthusiasts had moved away from our table. Some were at the bar. I couldn't see the others. But when I looked at Lihn again, there was an enthusiast with him, whispering something in his ear, before leaving the booth to find his friends, who were scattered around the establishment. And at that moment I knew that Lihn knew he was dead. My heart's given up on me, he said. It doesn't exist any more. Something's not right here, I thought. Lihn died of cancer, not a heart attack. An enormous heaviness was coming over me. So I got up and went to stretch my legs, but not in

Meeting With Enrique Lihn   195

the bar; I went out into the street. The sidewalks were gray and uneven and the sky looked like a mirror without a tain, the place where everything should have been reflected but where, in the end, nothing was. Nevertheless a feeling of normality prevailed and pervaded all vision. When I felt I'd had enough fresh air and it was time to get back to the bar, as I was climbing the three steps up to the door (stone steps, single blocks of a stone that had a granite-like consistency and the sheen of a gem), I ran into a guy who was shorter than me and dressed like a fifties gangster, a guy who had something of the caricature about him, the classic affable killer, who got me mixed up with someone he knew and greeted me, and I replied to his greeting although from the start I was sure that I didn't know him and that he was mistaken, but I behaved as if I knew him, as if I, too, had mixed him up with someone else, so the two of us greeted each other as we attempted ineffectively to climb those shining (yet lowly) stone steps, but the hit man's confusion lasted no more than a few seconds, he soon realized that he was mistaken, and then he looked at me in a different way, as if he were asking himself if I was confused too or if, on the contrary, I had been pulling his leg from the start, and since he was thick and suspicious (though sharp in his own paradoxical way), he asked me who I was, I remember, he asked me with a malicious smile on his lips, and I said, Shit, Jara, it's me, Bolaño, and it would have been clear to anyone from his smile that he wasn't Jara, but he played the game, as if suddenly, struck by a lightning bolt (and no, I'm not quoting one of Lihn's poems, much less one of mine), he fancied the idea of living the life of that unknown Jara for a minute or two, the Jara he would never be, except right there, stalled on the highest of those radiant steps, and he asked me about my life, he asked me (thick as a plank) who I was, admitting de facto that he was Jara, but a Jara who had forgotten the very existence of Bolaño, which is perfectly understandable after all, so I explained to him who I was, and, while I was at it, who he was too, thereby creating a Jara to suit me and him, that is, to suit that moment—an improbable, intelligent, courageous, rich, generous, daring Jara, in love with a beautiful woman and loved by her in return—and then the gangster smiled, more and more deeply convinced that I was making fun of him on but unable to bring the episode to a close and proceed to teach me a lesson, as if he had suddenly fallen in love with the image I was constructing for him, encouraging me to go on telling him not just about Jara but also about Jara's friends and finally the world, a world which seemed too wide even for Jara, a world in which even the great Jara was an ant whose death on a shining step would not have mattered at all to anyone, and then, at last, his friends appeared, two taller hit men wearing light-colored double-breasted suits, who looked at me and at the false Jara as if to ask him who I was, and he had no choice but to say it's Bolaño, and the two hit men greeted me, I shook their hands (rings, expensive watches, gold bracelets), and when they invited me to have a drink with them, I said, I can't, I'm with a friend, and pushed past Jara through the door and disappeared inside. Lihn was still in the booth. But now there were no enthusiasts to be seen in his vicinity. The glass was empty. He had taken the medicine and was waiting. Without saying a word we went up to his apartment. He lived on the seventh floor and we took the elevator, a very large elevator into which more than thirty people could have fitted. His apartment was rather small, especially for a Chilean writer, and there were no books.

To a question from me he replied that he hardly needed to read any more. But there are always books, he added. You could see the bar from his apartment. As if the floor were made of glass. I spent a while on my knees, watching the people down there, looking for the enthusiasts, or the three gangsters, but I could see only unfamiliar people, eating or drinking, but mostly moving from one table or booth to another, or up and down the bar, all seized by a feverish excitement, like characters in an early twentieth-century novel. After a while I reached the conclusion that something was wrong. If the floor of Lihn's apartment was glass and so was the roof of the bar, what about all the stories from the second to the sixth? Were they made of glass too? Then I looked down again and realized that between the first floor and the seventh floor there was nothing but empty space. This discovery distressed me. Jesus, Lihn, where have you brought me, I thought, though soon I was thinking, Jesus, Lihn, where have they brought you? I got to my feet carefully, because I knew that in that place, as opposed to the normal world, objects were more fragile than people, and I went looking for Lihn (who had disappeared) in the various rooms of the apartment, which didn't seem small any more, like a European writer's apartment, but spacious, enormous, like a writer's apartment in Chile, in the Third World, with cheap domestic help, and expensive, fragile objects, an apartment full of shifting shadows and rooms in semidarkness, in which I found two books, one a classic, like a smooth stone, the other modern, timeless, like shit, and gradually, as I looked for Lihn, I too began to grow cold, increasingly manic and cold, I started feeling ill, as if the apartment were turning on an imaginary axis, but then a door opened and I saw a swimming pool, and there was Lihn, swimming, and before I could open my mouth and say something about entropy, Lihn said that the bad thing about his medicine, the medicine he was taking to keep him alive, was that in a way it was turning him into a guinea pig for the drug company, words that I somehow expected to hear, as if the whole thing were a play and I had suddenly remembered my lines and the lines of my fellow actors, and then Lihn got out of the swimming pool and we went down to the ground floor, and we made our way through the crowded bar, and Lihn said: The tigers are finished, and: It was sweet while it lasted, and: You're not going to believe this, Bolaño, but in this neighborhood, only the dead go out for a walk. And by then we had reached the front of the bar and were standing at a window, looking at the streets and the façades of the buildings in that peculiar neighborhood where the only people out walking were dead. And we looked and looked, and the façades were clearly the façades of another time, like the sidewalks covered with parked cars, which also belonged to another time, a time that was silent yet mobile (Lihn was watching it move), a terrible time that endured for no reason other than sheer inertia.